"Woman, you were meant for loving," Josh said in a husky voice.

Mattie's heart thudded. His hand was on her throat and his dark eyes held a smoldering intensity that she hadn't seen before. His voice was raw with desire. The few times they had been together before their wedding, she'd sometimes wondered whether he'd seen her at all—but not now. At this moment she had his undivided attention.

"You are absolutely the first and only man to think so," she said.

He tilted her chin higher, running his index finger along her jaw in a slow, tantalizing trail that made her tingle. Her body was responding to him in ways she had never experienced. She felt as if she were wound tightly inside, an urgency gathering in her.

"It's been a hell of a long time since I really kissed a woman...."

MARRY ME,
Cowboy

HER TORRID
TEMPORARY
MARRIAGE
Sara Orwig

CONVENIENTLY
Wed

Silhouette Books

Published by Silhouette Books
America's Publisher of Contemporary Romance

SILHOUETTE BOOKS

ISBN 0-373-65325-5

HER TORRID TEMPORARY MARRIAGE

Copyright © 1998 by Sara Orwig

SARA ORWIG

lives in Oklahoma. She has a patient husband who will take her on research trips anywhere from big cities to old forts, and is an avid collector of Western history books. With a master's degree in English, Sara has written historical romance, mainstream fiction and contemporary romance. Books are beloved treasures that take Sara to magical worlds, and she loves both reading and writing them.

Please address questions and book requests to:
Silhouette Reader Service
U.S.: 3010 Walden Ave., P.O. Box 1325, Buffalo, NY 14269
Canadian: P.O. Box 609, Fort Erie, Ont. L2A 5X3

To Debra Robertson with thanks

One

"I wouldn't want to lose a wife—that's really rough. But otherwise, I wouldn't mind having your problem," Bear Holcomb said as he leaned against the bar and looked at Josh Brand.

"No, in my circumstances you wouldn't want it," Josh said to the hulking man who fit his nickname. "I'm not ready for a woman in my life. I just want a nanny for my baby, not an affair. I've had three nannies in less than two months. I wanted a nanny, and they wanted a husband."

"Stop advertising locally where they know who you are," Tom Shellene drawled, leaning back in a chair with his booted feet propped on a table and a beer in his hand, his shaggy blond hair hanging over his eyes. "These women know you're an eligible bachelor."

"I tried that," Josh replied, glancing around the

barroom at the empty, scarred tables. Afternoon sunlight streamed through the one narrow window that gave a limited view of the main street of Latimer, Texas. "I got ten replies—only two were worth interviewing. One woman talked two hours straight. The other one had child-rearing ideas that weren't compatible with what I want for my daughter." He took a long drink of cold beer and placed the bottle on the bar. "What happened to the little rosy-cheeked, gray-haired grannies like the one *I* had?"

"They've got careers or their own families," Bear drawled.

"So it seems." Josh smoothed errant wisps of blond hair on the six-month-old baby sleeping in a carrier at his elbow on the bar. He picked up the carrier. "I better clear out before Brad sees us and raises a fuss about a baby in a bar in his jurisdiction. See you guys. C'mon, Li'l Bit."

They mumbled goodbyes, and Josh stepped into warm Texas sunshine. The sun blazed high above the quiet main street. Light reflected off the chrome trim on pickups parked around the town square. The two-story sandstone county courthouse was bathed in a rosy hue, and tall mulberry trees shed circles of dappled shade over the courthouse lawn. Usually Josh loved the town, his ranch and springtime, but this year had turned into one nightmare after another, and now he barely noticed his surroundings.

He fastened Elizabeth Mary Brand's carrier onto the back seat of his black pickup and went around to climb behind the wheel.

"We're going home, Li'l Bit. Maybe this week's ad will find just the right nanny for you." He drove along the wide main street of the small town in Clayton County, on the edge of the hill country. In minutes they were heading northwest along the highway on the way to his Triple B ranch.

His thoughts churned, and he glanced at the sleeping baby, feeling love wash through him. She was so tiny, so fragile, yet he loved her fiercely and didn't want to give her up. His mother in Chicago would take Elizabeth, but he couldn't bear to part with her. Frustrated, he struck the steering wheel with his fist.

An hour later as he neared home, he swung around a curve and saw a blue pickup up ahead, pulled off on the wide shoulder beneath the shade of a cottonwood. The pickup was jacked up, a tire lying on the grass beside it. He put his foot on the brake to slow down. Turning to the baby, he said, "Li'l Bit, I may have to help my fellow man."

Then Josh noticed the driver, who was bending over, the faded jeans pulling tautly across her backside as she pulled the tire up onto its tread and rolled it to the wheel. Instantly he recognized the yellow pigtail and the longest pair of female legs in Clayton County.

"Well, Li'l Bit, I guess I don't have to offer my help. If I do offer, that self-sufficient cowgirl will take my head off." About fifty feet away he pressed down on the accelerator and watched his neighbor, Mattie Ryan, squat down and put the spare tire in place. Tossing her long blond braid over her shoulder, she started to replace the lug bolts.

"Oh, hell. Old habits die hard," he grumbled, and stomped on the brake to slow beside her and lower his window. "Hey, Mattie. Need help?"

She slanted him a look over her shoulder, her

thickly lashed green eyes gazing at him solemnly. "Hi, Josh. No, thanks."

"Okay," he said, closing the window and accelerating once again. Down the road a ways he glanced in his rearview mirror to see her pick up the flat tire and toss it into the bed of the pickup. "Now there's a lady, Li'l Bit, who wouldn't want an affair."

His eyes narrowed as he pictured Mattie Ryan in his mind. Almost six feet tall, she was full-bodied, long-legged and as independent as a barn cat. And sour on men. He remembered vague rumors about her getting dumped by a boyfriend in college, but he wasn't certain about details.

He and Mattie had grown up on neighboring ranches, established by their great-grandfathers. Josh's dad and Old Man Ryan were always battling each other, but they were civil to each other when out in public. Mattie's mother died when she was ten years old, and Frank Ryan had raised Mattie like the son he never had. Mattie had to be around twenty-eight or twenty-nine. She had two younger sisters who had long ago left the area and never returned.

Now Frank Ryan was dead, and Mattie had her grandmother to care for and the Rocking R ranch to run. And he heard she had been having financial troubles lately because of her father's illness and death.

Josh drove home mechanically, plans and possibilities involving his neighbor revolving in his mind.

Later that night he decided to give at least three weeks of thought to his ideas while he scrambled around trying to work and help his cook, Rosalie Benson, take care of Elizabeth at the same time. At the end of a week and a half, feeling desperate, he called

and made an appointment with Mattie, telling her he
wanted to discuss business.

As she was replacing a harness in the tack room of
the barn, Mattie heard a car motor. She strode out of
the barn in time to see a shiny black pickup approach-
ing the house, a plume of dust dancing in the pickup's
trail. Her heart missed a beat while she clamped her
jaw grimly. It was Josh Brand's pickup. And Gran was
in town and wouldn't be in the house to let him in.

Feeling her long braid flop against her back, Mattie
jogged toward the house as Josh's pickup swept
around the curve in front and disappeared from view.

With each step anger pulsed in her, because she
could guess why he had come. His would be the fourth
offer to buy her out since Dad died. She clenched her
fists. She could run this ranch! Her daddy had raised
her to take over when he was no longer able to run it.
As long as Gran was alive, she wasn't going to sell,
and she wasn't going to lose her home because of bad
weather or diseased cattle or a big loan. And not because of any man trying to coax her into selling. The
day would come when she would sell, but it wasn't
now.

When she rounded the corner, Josh Brand stood on
her porch with his hands on his hips while he waited
for her to answer the door. Her pulse skittered, and
she mentally swore. At twenty-eight she was six years
younger than Josh Brand, and in all the years she'd
known him he had never once seemed aware of her
as a female. Nor were most other males in the county
aware of her as a female. Which was quite all right.
She had grown accustomed to the hurt when she had

been thirteen and towered over all the boys her own age. But she hadn't towered over Josh, and he had set her pulse racing in a manner she couldn't control and didn't like. Still did. He might not be aware of her, but she was too aware of him.

His black hair was caught behind his head with a strip of rawhide, and his wide-brimmed black hat was pushed back on his head. His Kiowa heritage showed in his dark hair, eyes and skin, his prominent cheek-bones, his imperious straight nose. Her gaze ran across his broad shoulders and down the length of his lean body. "Josh!" she called as she jogged toward the house.

Josh turned to watch Mattie. She was graceful in a coltish way, her long legs stretching over the ground, her breasts swinging beneath the blue cotton shirt. He felt queasy, his stomach churning. The woman was an unknown quantity and formidable. Half the men in town were scared of her. She could be as forceful as her ornery dad, and for the hundredth time Josh wondered whether or not he was doing the right thing. His gaze ran over her in a practiced assessment. She was a lot of female and looked as healthy as his best horse.

Mattie took the steps two at a time, glanced up to see Josh's eyes raking over her. Her anger rose another notch while a flush burned her cheeks. Self-conscious about her dusty work clothes, she clenched her fists. "Did you want to see me?"

At the top step she paused and looked up—a unique experience. She knew Josh was taller than she was, but she hadn't been this close to him before and hadn't realized exactly how much taller he was. His dark eyes studied her with an intensity that took her breath. The

Brands were a tough bunch, and she suspected he was going to try to pressure her into selling the place by making her an offer that would be damned tempting.

She lifted her chin and stared back at him without blinking, wondering which one of them would blink or look away first. "Shall we go inside?" she asked.

"Any time."

They stood in silence, and she realized he was as aware of the contest of wills as she. She inhaled deeply. When his gaze dropped to her bosom, her anger soared, even though he had been the first to look away. She met his dark gaze again and thought she could detect a flash of amusement, but it was gone in seconds.

She reached for the door, and he bent down. For the first time she saw the baby carrier, a diaper bag and a sleeping baby. She knew he had a child and that he had lost his wife in a car wreck this past year, but she supposed he had someone to care for the baby. It startled her to see him carrying the baby with him.

"That's yours?" she asked, and then realized how ridiculous the question was. "Well, of course, I guess it is." She felt rattled and more annoyed than ever with him for causing her discomfort. "You wouldn't have someone else's baby." She couldn't remember whether it was a boy or girl. Judging from the pink dress, she assumed it was a girl.

"Come inside," she said, leading the way into the cool hallway. The floor shone with polish, and their boots clicked against the bare wood as she led Josh and his baby past the living room with its bulky, dark furniture. They passed the large family room, and she led the way into the small room that was her office at the southwest corner of the house.

She motioned to a straight-backed chair and walked around her oak desk, hoping to keep things as businesslike as possible and get him out of her house as quickly as she could. Her gaze ran over the familiar glass-fronted bookcases, the hat tree, the green leather chairs. "Have a seat. Would you like something to drink?"

"No, thanks." He set the carrier on the chair next to him and sat down, dropping his hat and the baby bag on the floor. As she sat behind the desk, she was disconcerted. Josh's piercing dark eyes made her feel nervous, female and vulnerable. And she hated feeling that way. She glanced around the room again, her gaze pausing a moment on the large map of the ranch hanging on the east wall. She reminded herself that she was owner of one of the largest ranches in the area and that the man across from her shouldn't intimidate her. She tried to ignore the fact that she found him handsome as sin, and she wished her pulse would quiet to a normal rate.

"Now, what did you want to see me about?"

"You get right to the point, don't you?" he asked. This time there was no mistaking the amusement in his voice.

"Why on earth would we do otherwise?" she snapped, annoyed that he made her uneasy. He was too masculine, too *appealing*. "We don't have much to chitchat about."

"We're neighbors, Mattie. We should get to be friends."

"I think it's three generations too late for that," she

said, still flustered by him and annoyed with herself. What was it about Josh Brand that made her come unglued? With other men she could stay cool and collected. Embarrassed, she realized how unfriendly her statement sounded and added, "Well, I guess we could try to be friends." Knowing men had no interest in striking up a friendship with her, she tilted her head to look at him. "But I don't think that's why you called me."

"No, it's not," he admitted, still studying her as if she was a prime bit of horseflesh that he was considering purchasing. He placed one booted foot on his knee. He looked relaxed as if this were his office and she was the visitor. "My wife was killed four months ago in a car wreck," he announced gruffly.

"I remember hearing that, and I'm sorry," she said, shocked to see the pain in his eyes. She knew how much the loss of a loved one hurt, but Josh Brand had always seemed invincible. She was startled that he was still so obviously suffering from his loss. "At least you have your baby."

He nodded and glanced at the sleeping child. "I want to keep Elizabeth," he said, and his voice became more gravelly. His dark gaze returned to Mattie. "That's why I'm here." As he stared at her, she had a premonition of disaster. She couldn't imagine why or what his loss had to do with her. Maybe he wanted to sell his place to her. The thought startled her, and her mind raced. With a sinking feeling, she knew she could never buy it. She was strapped for money as it was, and worried about how she was going to keep the Rocking R going. Josh Brand had a marvelous ranch. In her mind she pictured the rolling fields and the cattle she knew he owned.

"Mattie, I've tried to hire nannies and I can't find one who is remotely satisfactory."

"I'm sorry to hear that," she said, puzzled. The man had lost his mind if he had come to hire *her* as a nanny.

Josh stared at the woman across the desk. Reluctance held his tongue. He knew once the words were out of his mouth, he couldn't take them back. He clenched and unclenched his fists and looked again at Elizabeth who was blissfully sleeping, unaware of the turmoil and anguish of her father.

His gaze swung back to Mattie. Big green eyes stared at him, and the fleeting thought crossed his mind that the woman's face was pretty. He inhaled, realizing the train of thought and knowing that it didn't matter whether she looked like Attila or Cleopatra. Her looks were beside the point.

"How do you feel about children?" he blurted, wondering when he had lost all finesse.

She blinked, looking startled, then glanced at Elizabeth. "They're nice," she replied cautiously, sounding curious and staring at him intently.

"Yeah. Mattie, I can't find a nanny, and I've come to make a proposition to you."

"Oh, if you think I would hire out as a nanny—oh, no! I couldn't ever—"

He held up a hand and shook his head. "Of course not."

Startled, she bit her lip and stared at him. "If you're not suggesting I be a nanny, what are you suggesting?" she asked, her curiosity running rampant because he looked as if he was going to faint. Sweat beaded on his forehead, and he was ashen in spite of his dark skin. She had seen Josh Brand in fights when he was young and she had seen him bronc riding in rodeos. He was as tough as her father, yet he looked as if he was coming apart right before her eyes. "Are you all right?"

"I'm fine." When his compelling dark eyes met hers, she felt threatened, as if whatever this man wanted from her, she was going to have the fight of her life to keep from giving in to him.

"How are your sisters?"

"They're fine," Mattie answered, becoming more puzzled.

"I understand Carlina is married and lives in Denver and won't come back home."

"That's right. Neither she nor Andrea will ever come back here to live," she said. "Pardon me for asking but aren't we drifting from why you're here?"

"Not exactly." He leaned forward, placing his elbows on his knees, his feet squarely on the floor. "Our ranches adjoin. As I understand it, your sisters won't be returning to live here and don't want the ranch. You don't have any heirs, no husband."

"I'm not selling," she announced frostily, drawing herself up, feeling icy inside. "My sisters have said I can deal with the ranch as I see fit. I can manage their shares. I run this ranch, and it's not on the market. Not now, not tomorrow, not because I've lost my dad."

"I'm not buying."

She opened her mouth to continue, realized what he'd said and snapped her mouth closed. More confused than ever, she stared at him. He gripped the arms of the chair and his knuckles were white. "Then what do you want?" she asked.

"I want you to marry me."

Two

Stunned, Mattie stared at him, unable to speak. When she realized her mouth had dropped open, she closed it. "That's absolutely absurd!"

"Hear me out," he commanded in a tone of voice that made her close her mouth again.

Josh stared at her while his heart drummed. He was in deep now. He glanced at Elizabeth for reassurance and then returned his attention to Mattie, who was staring at him with wide-eyed alarm. If he had drawn a gun on her, he suspected she would have coolly tried to wrestle him to the ground for it, but his proposal must have frightened her as much as it did him. Somehow it reassured him to know that.

"I need a woman in the house. I don't want a wife in the fullest sense. I need a mother for Elizabeth, someone who is intelligent and strong and kind." Mattie's face flushed, and she blinked, and he wondered if she was startled that he thought she possessed those qualities.

"You don't know anything about me," she whispered.

"I've known about you all my life, the same as you know me. And I've asked around."

Pinpoints of fire flared in the depths of her eyes, and he spoke quickly before she could complain about his inquiring into her background.

"We could operate our ranches together. You'd be in charge of hiring a nanny for Elizabeth and seeing to Li'l Bit's upbringing. In return, you'd have my help, and you'd become part owner of my ranch. I'm willing to give you a share of my land in exchange."

Shocked speechless, she stared at him in silence, too stunned to think of a reply. Disconcerted, she ran her hand across her forehead. "That is absolutely preposterous! Just go hire a nanny and a cook."

"I have, and it didn't work out."

"Well, try again," she snapped impatiently. "You hire men to work for you. A nanny is the same sort of thing. Why didn't the nannies work out?"

His face flushed, and his gaze slid away. "So far, I can't find anyone grandmotherly, and the others— well, hellfire." His dark eyes met hers. "I'm not so damned appealing, but so far, the only ones I've hired want a permanent relationship."

"For heaven's sake, marry one of them!"

"They want the real thing," he said stonily. "They want more than I can give. I'm not going to love another woman." His voice became gravelly, and she could see the pain in his eyes as he battled his emotions. "I don't want to marry for love. I don't ever want that heartache again."

"I'm sorry," she said, seeing his pain and feeling sad over his loss.

He shrugged, then smoothed the baby's hair as if to reassure himself that he still had her. Mattie's sympathy mingled with her shock. It was obvious he thought she would be quite happy to settle for a celibate relationship that didn't involve heart or body, but merely an overseer of his household. She felt annoyed and flattered at the same time. And still shocked. And beneath all her shock, his words echoed in her mind, *Intelligent and strong and kind...* The praise was astounding. She glanced at the sleeping baby.

"I don't know one thing about a baby."

"You don't have to. You know calves and foals and how to run a ranch. You can hire a nanny. With you there, I won't have problems with one. You and I can work out a damned good business arrangement if you stop to think about it. You'll be gaining a lot of land—"

"So will you, actually."

"Yes, I will," he replied solemnly. "You don't have any heirs. The danger, as I see it, is that you might fall in love someday and want to marry. We could annul the marriage and break the ranches back up. I would want a prenuptial agreement to protect Elizabeth's inheritance. Also, I wouldn't want you to bring any scandal to her, but I don't think you would."

"This is absolutely ridiculous! I'll run an ad and hire you a nanny and you can forget marriage."

He leaned forward another few inches, running his hand over his head. His fingers were long and blunt, the nails closely trimmed. She glanced at his face, and his dark eyes snagged and held her attention. "I know I've shocked you. I'm desperate and I've had time to think this over. You should give my proposal some thought. There are advantages to you. You have your grandmother to take care of. You've had a tough year, and your father's illness ran up big bills. You're still sending your sister Andrea to college—to medical school, from what I understand."

Annoyed, Mattie frowned. "You've been snooping into my life," she complained, only half thinking about what she was saying while his proposal spun in her mind. Josh Brand wanted her—Mattie Ryan, the Clayton County spinster—to marry him. Impossible! Shock held her in a vacuum, and she had to force her attention to what he was saying.

"Everyone in these parts knows about each other's business. This community is close. Everyone knows everyone. You know a lot about my life."

"Maybe, but I don't know *you*. We can't marry. We're strangers."

"I'm not talking about a real marriage. If you want the physical side, I can do that, I suppose, but my heart is as numb as that desk."

Agitated, she stood and went to the window to look at the rolling land that belonged to her. What Josh proposed was impossible. She couldn't even imagine herself in any kind of marriage to him, even the most platonic relationship.

"Josh, I'm sorry, but I have my life." She turned to face him. "I don't know babies or how to be a wife. I'm flattered that you asked—"

"Mattie, I've been asking questions. Your dad

mortgaged a large section of the Rocking R. You have some big debts.''

''Dammit! No one in this county can keep his mouth shut from the banker on down to—''

''Come over for dinner tonight,'' Josh said abruptly, interrupting her. ''Let's get to know each other better.''

At a loss for words, she stared at him in silence.

''Just dinner, Mattie. Not scared of me, are you?''

''No! All right,'' she answered, her heart fluttering. She felt lost. She had never dated seriously, never flirted or had casual relationships with boyfriends. She had worked with men all her life, but she had never had personal relationships with any man. Josh Brand was just the opposite. She could remember from school functions, football games and rodeos that Josh had had females fluttering around him since he was a little kid. And she remembered his beautiful, sophisticated wife.

''Good. I'll come pick you up about seven.''

Elizabeth stirred and let out a wail. He turned and unbuckled her, then picked her up out of the carrier, talking softly to her. Mattie stared at him, watching the transformation of this man who was so masculine and tough. He cradled the baby, cooing to her as he jiggled her and tried to calm her. His voice gentled, his features softened; he looked incredibly appealing, no longer formidable. He fumbled in the diaper bag and produced a bottle, which the baby grasped and yanked into her mouth, her large brown eyes watching him constantly.

''There's my girl,'' he said, smoothing her hair. ''Elizabeth, this is Mattie. Mattie, this is Elizabeth.''

"She's sweet," Mattie said perfunctorily. "I've never been around babies."

"I hadn't, either. They'll put up with a lot," he said without taking his gaze from his daughter.

"I really don't think—"

He raised his head, his eyes focusing on Mattie with a look that made her pause. Without taking his gaze from her, he crossed the room, closing the distance between them. Her pulse jumped as she watched him stop only inches from her. He stood too close. She could detect the scent of aftershave, of talcum, of milk. The baby made soft sucking sounds while he held her bottle, and Mattie glanced at her. Elizabeth's fingers were incredibly tiny and dainty, her dark lashes long and thick, and she had beautiful rosy skin. Mattie's gaze lifted to meet Josh's again, causing another leap in her pulse.

As he leaned closer, she noticed the faint stubble on his jaw, his thick black lashes. He shook his head. "Don't act in haste," he said in a low voice. "Come have dinner and we'll talk some more. Think about what you have to gain...and what you have to lose."

"I think you have the most to lose. You may fall in love again."

His eyes were direct and unblinking as he shook his head. "Never again. I adored Lisa. With those marriage-hungry nannies, I felt as if a noose were closing around my neck. But I need someone for Elizabeth and if you agree to do this for me and for her, I'll do right by you."

"That's easy to say now."

"Think about what you want in a prenuptial agreement. You ask for high stakes, and you'll see how sincere I am and how much I intend to stand by what I promise.'' He stared at her a moment in silence while her heart pounded like galloping hoofbeats. ''I'll see you at seven.''

He turned, put on his hat and was halfway to the door before she realized it. As she looked at his broad shoulders, she felt dazed. He held the carrier and baby bag in one hand, the baby in the other.

''I'll help carry something,'' she said, catching up with him and taking the carrier and bag.

They walked outside to his pickup where he turned to take the carrier from her. His fingers brushed hers, and she felt an electric tingle from the contact. Why was she so aware of him? She watched him set the carrier on the back seat of the truck.

''Can you hold her a minute?'' he asked, thrusting the baby into her arms without waiting for her answer. The moment the bottle left Elizabeth's mouth, she screwed up her face and began to protest with a loud wail. He gave the baby her bottle, and her tiny hands closed on it. Mattie looked at the small, warm bundle in her arms. Two little dark eyes seemed to stare right through her with the same directness as her father's.

When she looked at the baby, Mattie was frightened and uncertain. She couldn't be responsible for this tiny person. Panic gripped her, and her gaze lifted from the infant to her father. Josh leaned into the car, his jeans pulling over his muscled legs while he buckled the carrier into the pickup.

Turning, he said, ''Come here, Li'l Bit,'' his usual no-nonsense bass voice changing again to a gentleness that made Mattie melt. He took the baby from Mattie. ''I'll pick you up tonight.''

After he strapped Elizabeth in securely, he strode around the pickup, climbed behind the wheel and was gone, roaring down the road, sending dust spiraling up behind the pickup while she stared in shock.

Marriage. Josh Brand wanted her to *marry* him. It was unbelievable, impossible, amazing. And at one time in her life, she would have been ecstatic. Now she was older and more realistic. What the man needed to do was continue advertising for nannies, hire a nice, reliable one and then wait. Later, he would marry a woman he truly loved.

She shook her head, catching her braid and pulling it across her shoulder to brush the ends of it with her fingers. Turning around, her gaze swept the ranch: the long, low barn, the corral, the bunkhouse, the other outbuildings, but her thoughts were on the man driving away.

She had a date with Josh Brand for dinner. She felt as if life had turned topsy-turvy. Why would he ask her to marry him? *I need a mother for Elizabeth, someone who is intelligent and strong and kind....* The words dazzled her until she faced reality. Josh Brand had never paid the least bit of attention to her before. He wanted a glorified nanny to be in charge of the real nanny. Mattie clamped her jaw closed and strode back into the house. She couldn't do that, but she had agreed to the dinner, so there was no escaping the evening with him. Now she had to worry about what to wear.

And when she told Gran what she was doing, all hell would break loose. Gran thought she should be married and was constantly trying to get her to socialize more in town. As if it would do her any good.

She had grown up in this county, and none of the men had ever wanted to date her. Until now. She shook her head and entered the house, going directly to the closet in her bedroom.

At six forty-five Mattie paced the forty-foot living room. Usually the house was a haven of comfort with its familiar cowhide and maple furniture, but tonight her stomach churned.

"Mattie, for corn's sake, sit down!" Irma Ryan stared at her granddaughter. "And I think you should take your hair out of that infernal braid and wear a dress."

"I feel more comfortable in jeans," Mattie remarked, locking her fingers together nervously, looking at her diminutive, white-haired grandmother and idly wondering why all the other females in the Ryan family were under five and a half feet tall. Irma was dwarfed by the old maple rocking chair. Her feet, clad in sneakers, were propped on a lower rung, the white toes peeping out beneath the hem of jeans.

"I don't think you should be ready and waiting. Let Josh come sit and talk with me awhile."

"All he wants to do is talk business. He's interested in acquiring part of the ranch."

"Nonsense! He wouldn't ask you to dinner at his house if all he wanted was to try to buy some land. Mattie, you should listen to me."

Mattie's conscience hurt. She couldn't recall ever lying to Gran in her life, but she also couldn't bring herself to tell Gran that Josh Brand had asked her to marry him. Gran would be planning the wedding down to the last detail.

"I hear a car," Mattie said, going to the front window to shift a lace curtain and look at the black pickup coming up the road toward the house. Why did she feel destiny was driving full tilt to her door?

"Go back to your room, and Lottie will let him in. That's her job."

In spite of her nervousness, Mattie laughed. "You and Lottie both want to look him over."

"Of course we do," Gran admitted. "Lottie's worked for us since you were a baby. She's like a mother to you, and she'd like to see the man who wants to take you out."

"It's not that big a deal."

"Mattie, don't you dare leave without bringing him in here to see me. Now humor your granny and go to your room and let me talk to him. I haven't really had ten words with a good-looking young man in years."

"And you don't need to start tonight."

"Please," Irma said, gazing through her bifocals with wide blue eyes. "I don't get to do many things I enjoy."

Mattie threw up her hands and left the room. Her grandmother got to do plenty that she enjoyed, from chewing tobacco to playing poker in town on Saturday afternoons with a bunch of old codgers.

When the bell chimed, Lottie Needham hurried from the kitchen. Her gray hair was a cap of curls around a rosy face, and she smiled at Mattie. "I know Miz Ryan wants to meet your beau."

"Oh, for heaven's sake, Lottie, he's not my beau!" Mattie paused and bit her lip, waving her hand at the short, stout woman who was like part of the family. "Go ahead and get the door. I'll be in my room."

Mattie hurried upstairs and down the hall, going to the window to look down at the black pickup. She turned, glancing again in the mirror. She had scrubbed and washed her hair and tried on half a dozen different outfits, deciding in exasperation to dress like she would any other night. She wore jeans, a blue shirt and had braided her hair. And she had only the tiniest bit more makeup than she always wore. How could she spend the evening with Josh? She didn't know how to make small talk, and all he wanted was a business deal that she could not agree to. Wiping her damp palms against her jeans, she went downstairs.

Halfway down the stairs she heard Josh's voice and his laughter. Now what had Gran said to make him laugh? Then Gran burst out laughing.

"You two sound as if you are enjoying yourselves," Mattie said, entering the room. "Evening, Josh."

He unfolded his long frame from the sofa and stood, his dark gaze sweeping over her in a manner that made her skin tingle. He had changed clothes since earlier in the day. As she expected, he was in jeans. He wore a navy shirt with the sleeves turned back. His long black hair was tied behind his head with a bit of rawhide. He was darkly handsome; a devil in blue jeans trying to buy her soul. In spite of that, her pulse jumped at the sight of him. Whether she liked it or not, he stirred a primitive reaction in her. At the same time, her awareness of him made her doubly nervous in his presence.

"Hi, Mattie," he said quietly. "If you're ready, we'll be going. Irma, I enjoyed talking to you."

"You come again," Gran said happily.

"I intend to," he answered with equal cheer. He took Mattie's arm lightly as they left the room. Their boots scraped the polished hardwood floor, and as they passed the floor-to-ceiling gilt-framed mirror she glanced at their image, shocked again at how tall he was. She usually towered over men or was at least their height. But not Josh. His size and strength were impressive.

"You look pretty," he said quietly, and she glanced up.

"Thank you," she answered, without believing he really meant what he'd said.

They left the house and crossed the porch, descending the steps to his pickup where he opened the door for her. She reached for the handle at the same moment, and her hand closed over his.

"Sorry," she said, flushing, wondering if he had any idea how seldom she had been out with a man. She climbed inside the pickup, then watched him go around and slide behind the wheel.

"Your grandmother is interesting. I can't remember ever talking to her much before."

"She's a character. She's had two heart attacks, and it's still a shock to realize that she outlived my dad. I always thought I would have him forever."

"Yeah, I know," Josh answered gruffly, and she realized she had struck a nerve and he was probably thinking about his wife.

"Sorry. I didn't mean to remind you of your loss."

"That's all right. I have to live with it."

"Where's Elizabeth?"

"Rosalie, my cook, is watching her tonight."

"Why don't you get Rosalie to be a nanny as well as a cook?"

"How I wish! Rosalie is getting up in years, and her kids bought her a condo in Arizona. She's leaving next month."

Mattie felt awkward and uncomfortable and too aware of the man beside her. Her gaze ran over the rugged planes of his face, his strong cheekbones, his mouth that was faintly chapped, yet as appealing as the rest of him. He exuded an aura of self-confidence that increased her nervousness. Afraid he would catch her staring, she turned to look at the land flashing past them, the stands of oaks on the hillsides, the fresh arrival of spring wildflowers. "We got a lot of rain last week," she remarked.

"Glad to have it. You've got good water on your land with Cotton Creek."

"Yes, thank heaven," she replied, knowing she had better water resources than he did and wondering if that was a large part of what prompted his proposal.

"Josh, this really is impossible," she blurted nervously. The man tied her in knots. He was appealing, sexy, popular with everyone in the county—she didn't belong with him.

"What's impossible?" he asked easily. "My proposal?"

"Yes. I don't think you've given enough thought to it." She fished in her pocket and withdrew a slip of paper. "I sat down and thought of the women I know who live here and can marry you."

He laughed, a throaty chuckle that sent tingles spiraling through her. "Did you now! How do you know what kind of woman I would like to marry?"

''You proposed to *me*—and I'm all but a stranger—
so you're obviously not particular.''

''I'm damned particular. I gave this a lot of thought
already,'' he said, shooting her a glance that made her
toes curl. Momentarily she forgot her list as she
thought about Josh Brand spending hours thinking
about her and considering her as marriage material.
Even if it was a loveless marriage, it still involved
getting emotionally entangled. The idea of emotional
entanglement with the man beside her took her breath
away.

''Well, go ahead. Who's on your list?'' he asked
with amusement.

She straightened the paper. ''How about Reba Tal-
madge?''

He shook his head. ''Too unreliable.''

''Reba?'' Reba lived in Latimer and was the town
librarian in Spencer, a neighboring town. As far as
Mattie knew, Reba was practical and reliable and
rather attractive. And she had just broken an engagement.

''All right, how about Candice Webster?''

''She was the first nanny. And no. Definitely not.''

Biting her lip, Mattie glanced at him. He gave her
one quick glance in return, and she looked into his
eyes filled with determination. When he returned his
gaze to the road, she noticed a muscle flexing in his
jaw.

''Alyssa Hagen?''

''Never. Woman never stops talking and has a laugh
that would drive a man to flight.''

Worried, Mattie ran her gaze over her list. The man
was damned particular! ''Barb Crandall?''

He reached over and withdrew the list from Mattie's fingers, balled it up and tossed it into a litter bag on the dash. "Thanks, anyway. I think I've made the best possible choice. And I've considered every female I've ever known."

Mattie bit her lip again and turned to look at the land. She was flattered, astonished, wondering if she would ever get over her amazement. And she was uneasy. She couldn't possibly marry Josh Brand. The notion was totally unthinkable. The man could have almost any woman he wanted. Why would he want her?

They rode in silence while her thoughts seethed. She should just outright ask him, but it was difficult. She couldn't even deal with him on this introductory level. It was beyond imagination to think about marrying him and dealing with him daily about everything in her life. And he disturbed her. She was intensely aware of him. He was too attractive, too incredibly masculine. She rubbed her damp palms together nervously.

"Relax, Mattie," he said quietly.

"It's difficult under the circumstances."

"We're just going to a simple dinner and discuss our futures."

She didn't reply and watched the sun slanting in the sky, shadows growing slightly longer, until he turned onto his ranch road. Too soon to suit her, his sprawling ranch house came into view. She couldn't recall having seen his home before. The house was long. The overhang of the sloping roof covered a porch that circled the house. Pots of flowers hung from the roof and more pots with bright red hibiscus stood on the porch.

A hummingbird darted among the flowers. Beyond the house were various structures: a barn twice the size of hers, a corral, a bunkhouse, a shop, another building that might be an office, two small buildings. She saw a tractor in a shed and another pickup parked in front of the three-stall garage. The buildings were in good shape, and the place appeared thriving and welcoming. Josh parked the truck and came around to open the door.

"C'mon. I'll show you the house. Rosalie took Elizabeth to her house. It's just down that road a ways," he said, pointing to a road that angled off from the house and disappeared between stands of oaks.

Nervous, Mattie climbed out of the pickup and followed him across the porch. He opened the back door and waited while she entered the kitchen.

"How about a beer? Wine? Iced tea?"

"Tea sounds good," she said as she looked around at the oak cabinets and terrazzo floor. The room was spacious and inviting, the aroma of hot bread still hovering in the air. On the tile counter she saw two pans with golden loaves swelling over the sides.

He handed her a glass of iced tea. "Sugar or lemon?"

"No, thanks."

He set his cold beer on the kitchen table and moved closer, resting his hands lightly on her shoulders. The warmth of his hands kindled a responding warmth in her. She was intensely aware of him, suspecting he thought nothing of the casual touch of his hands on her or his standing so close to her.

"Mattie, relax. You look as if I'm the devil and I've asked you to sell your soul."

"That's sort of how I see you. Your proposal shocked me, and I think you should find a nanny and forget a loveless marriage," she said, noticing his thick lashes, his sculpted lips. When he moved close to her, his presence made her more nervous than ever.

"Come look at my house," he urged in a coaxing voice that she couldn't resist.

She nodded, and he moved away. Even though the kitchen was spacious, he dominated it with his height and broad shoulders and his raw masculinity. Her gaze slid down his back to his slim hips, and her mouth went dry.

He turned to slant her a curious glance. "Are you with me?"

"Yes!" Burning with embarrassment because he had caught her studying his hips, she caught up and walked beside him into a large, comfortable family room, in forest green and brown decor, with a stone fireplace. A game table stood in one corner and an antique rifle was mounted above the fireplace. The furniture was large, as if it had been selected for a tall man. She crossed the room to a wall paneled in knotty pine and covered with pictures.

"That's the rogues' gallery," Josh remarked, coming to stand beside her, his shoulder lightly brushing hers. "Here's great-grandpa Daniel Brand."

"Who tried to kill my great-grandfather," she said with amusement as she moved closer to look at the faded picture of a bearded man with a beak of a nose above a thick mustache.

"I think it was the other way around," Josh replied lightly, and she laughed.

"At least by the time our fathers took over the

ranches, they weren't shooting at each other. They just didn't speak unless they had to.''

"That's Daniel's rifle mounted over the fireplace. He made that table," Josh said, pointing to a sturdy, simple table that had nicks in the legs from hard use. He pointed to a picture of horses on the opposite wall. "My grandfather hung that picture. It was his favorite, so we've always kept it. The little rocker was my grandmother's chair."

"Your roots go back like my family's." Mattie moved along the row of pictures, examining another faded photograph of a dark-skinned, black-haired woman and Daniel Brand.

"That was Daniel's wife, Little Star. She was full-blood Kiowa."

"She's a beautiful woman."

"We have more Kiowa blood. Here's the next generation. Grandpa Isaac was a half-breed. He married Summer Setaingia, another full-blood—here's her picture," Josh said, pointing to another husband-wife portrait that bore a family resemblance to Josh in their dark eyes and hair and prominent cheekbones. Mattie gazed at the pictures, but she was more aware of the tall man standing so close beside her, his body lightly touching hers. She walked along, gazing at pictures until she came to one that featured a small boy with brown eyes, flowing black hair and a cocky grin. She knew it had to be Josh. "This is you."

"Yeah. Mom put these up. I've never bothered changing them, nor did Lisa."

"This is the house you grew up in?"

"Yes. This room and the first two bedrooms are the original house that my great-grandpa Daniel built. Dad redid the kitchen and added the other rooms. After Dad died, Mom remarried and moved to Chicago. When Lisa and I married, we moved in here. Lisa had the house remodeled, but she didn't change much in this room or the dining room. The dining room table was my grandfather's. And there are a few old tables here that belonged to great-grandpa Daniel.''

"Sounds like our house.''

They moved to an adjoining formal living room that had an off-white carpet and the same forest green color in the upholstered furniture. "Lisa did this room over. I'm hardly ever in it,'' he said in a flat voice, and Mattie realized that every time he mentioned his wife, he sounded pained.

She followed him into a dining room that held a long mahogany table with twelve chairs. A silver tea service gleamed on the polished sideboard. "You have a nice home.''

"Thanks. The bedrooms are down the hall,'' he said casually. "Want to sit outside with me while I grill steaks?''

"Sure,'' she answered, thinking both of them had roots that went far back in time. Their backgrounds were the same, but there the similarities ended.

He returned to the kitchen to get a platter of steaks, and they stepped outside to a deck where he motioned toward lawn chairs. "Sit down while I cook these. Rosalie already prepared potatoes and carrots, so dinner'll be ready soon.''

As soon as the steaks were on, he pulled a chair close and sat down facing her.

"You really have a beautiful place,'' she remarked.

"The ranch has done well. I hear you just acquired two new quarter horses from Ed Williams's stables."

"I'm trying to improve our stock."

"That should do it." He studied her, and every time he gave her one of his long intense looks, she felt ensnared and at a disadvantage, as if he were trying to see into her soul and succeeding. "You don't object to my Indian blood, do you?"

"Of course not," she replied, startled.

He shrugged broad shoulders. "I didn't think you would, but some might. I run into occasional prejudice."

"It isn't *you* who's causing my objections to your proposal—it's me. I don't know anything about babies."

"It doesn't take long to learn," he replied in an off-handed tone as if the whole matter were settled in his mind. She wondered how many things in his life didn't go the way he wanted. He had lost his wife and father, but other than that, she suspected he usually did what he wanted and got what he wanted.

He went to the grill, and she watched him turn the steaks, her gaze running down his back to his narrow waist, over his trim backside. *Her husband?* Impossible! Her pulse skittered at the thought.

In minutes they sat down in the kitchen to thick steaks, baked potatoes, crisp steamed carrots with slices of homemade bread.

"You're a good cook."

"Thanks, but Rosalie gets most of the credit. I don't do bread. Are you riding in the July rodeo?"

She shook her head. "I don't participate as much as I used to. How about you?"

"I'll be in calf roping."

They discussed ranch life, and she felt as if her nerves were stretching to a breaking point. She wanted to get to the subject, decline his offer and go home to her peaceful life. Even if it was lonely. Yet the man across the table from her was handsome and charming. A tiny bubbling excitement tugged at her, and she tried to ignore it.

When they finished eating, he refused to let her help him clean up. "It should be cooler out now. Let's walk, and I'll show you the barn."

She nodded, although she was tempted to give a firm no to his proposal and go home. She suspected he wanted to show off his ranch, but she didn't dare give a thought to becoming part of it.

The sun was slanting toward the western horizon when they went outside, and a slight breeze had sprung up. His house was a fenced oasis with a green lawn and beds of blooming flowers. Sprinklers slowly revolved, sending sparkling silver streams over the grass. Two tall live oaks spread branches above the lawn, creating cool shade in the late hours. A picket fence surrounded the backyard, and they followed a winding walk toward the gate.

"Why can't your mother come stay for a time until you hire a nanny?"

"Mom is busy. My stepfather is Thornton Bridges. He's a state representative, and he has his sights set on running for the Senate next election. They have a busy social life, and Mom is into a lot of charities. She'd be glad to take Elizabeth to Chicago, but I don't want to give up my daughter."

Breezes tugged at Mattie's hair as she lifted her face

and gazed across his rolling land. In the distance she could see a herd of white-faced Herefords grazing. They left a flagstone path, went through a gate and followed the wide, graveled driveway toward the large barn. A collie came bounding up, frisking around Josh.

"Down, Grady," he said gently, and the dog fell into step behind them.

She glanced at Josh surreptitiously, unable to imagine why he had selected her in spite of what he had told her. He had so many choices. Suddenly the butterflies in her stomach were back, fluttering wildly. Dinner was over, and she had to tell him no, for once and for all time.

They walked through the spacious barn, where Josh showed her the tack room, and then they strolled to a fenced pasture where mares were grazing. They stood beside the fence to look at the horses that were as fine as any she owned. Josh leaned against the fence and turned to face her. He caught her braid in his hand and toyed with it, the tugs against her scalp too faint to be the cause of the tingles she experienced. She wanted to back up because he was standing so close.

"I gave thought to what I wanted before I asked you, Mattie," he said quietly. His brown eyes were compelling as he searched her gaze.

She looked up at him and realized again that he was one of the few men she had known in her life who made her feel petite. "It's just impossible. I don't know anything about babies. I really don't know anything about men, either."

"You work with men daily. You have all your life."

"I've never dated, and that's different," she said,

feeling her nervousness increase. Her skin felt prickly, and she was too conscious of him.

"It doesn't matter one iota to me that you've never dated. And I doubt if *never* is the correct description. You've dated some," he said. "You dated in college."

"Very little, and it meant nothing. I feel like I'm an anachronism, a real throwback to another age and time when there were women like me. I've never seriously dated anyone."

Josh wondered about the stories he had heard. She was skittish as a colt around him, but he suspected it was because of his proposal, not the fact that she was out with a man. Her gaze remained on the mares. Only the pink that suffused her cheeks gave a hint to her feelings.

"I thought you dated someone seriously in college. That's what I heard."

The corner of her mouth lifted slightly in a wry smile. "Then you heard wrong. Gran might have started a rumor because she has always wanted me to find a man—but no, I didn't. I'm taller than most men I know. Growing up I was a tomboy. Sometimes I think I scare some men."

"You don't scare me," Josh said quietly, wondering about her, realizing maybe she had been hurt by the boys she had grown up with. And he wondered how much her father had kept men away.

Josh's gaze roamed over her profile, her wide brow, the thick blond hair, her big eyes and full rosy lips. His gaze dropped to her slender throat and full breasts that thrust tautly against her blue shirt. The woman was more than attractive. Surprised at himself, he studied her more closely. She was a good-looking woman, but he had never really noticed her before. And he was amazed how he noticed her now. It was the first time he had really looked at a woman since Lisa's death.

"You work with men. You ride in rodeos. If you haven't dated, it's been your choice some of the time." Another blush deepened the color of her cheeks, and he saw that he was right.

"Maybe so."

He caught her thick braid and tugged on it slightly to get her to look at him. As she turned her head, he looked into guileless green eyes that held tiny gold flecks in the center. "You don't have to know men or have dated. Our marriage wouldn't be much different from your life now except we'll be under one roof and you'll be in charge of Elizabeth's nanny. I don't care about a physical relationship. I wouldn't ever force myself on you. I'll give you all the room you want."

Another blush, this time fiery, turned her throat and cheeks red. "I can't imagine the arrangement you're suggesting, and I think within six months from now, you would regret it terribly."

"You're wrong. I've given this a lot of thought."

"Besides a sham marriage being something you shouldn't rush into, there's another reason for me to say no. I'll tell you something I've never told anyone else. I wouldn't ever tell Gran, as a matter of fact."

Mattie paused, and he wondered what deep secret she was about to reveal to him. He was still thinking about her as an appealing woman. Why hadn't anyone dated her? He decided it definitely had to have been her choice most of the time.

''What haven't you told anyone?'' he prompted, wondering what secret she harbored.

Her green eyes went beyond him as if she were gazing into the horizon. ''Someday I hope to sell the ranch and get far away from here.''

Stunned by her admission, feeling a sudden painful stab of guilt for trying to involve her in a plan that was to his advantage, he dropped her braid. As he looked down at her, he felt all his plans crumbling to pieces.

Three

"**Y**ou don't want this?" he asked, waving his hand and feeling astounded. "I figured you would live and breathe and sleep ranching. That's all you've ever done. What else do you want?"

"My father always relied on me, and he brought me up to carry on when he was gone. But I want something else."

"Lord, generations of your family lived on that ranch! You'd just let it all go?"

She raised her chin, her eyes flashing fire, and he guessed that when Mattie made up her mind, she could be mule stubborn. "My sisters left without a qualm. If my family is all gone except me, why do I have to preserve a heritage that I no longer want?"

"It's hard to imagine you don't want it," he said, thinking about some of his arguments with Lisa over his staying on a ranch.

"I would never have done anything to hurt Dad, but ranch life isn't all I want. He never asked me. He just assumed. He let my sisters go. By the time they were high school age, they were in boarding schools, and they've never returned. Nor will they ever."

"Your father's gone now, so what's keeping you here?"

"I have Gran. I won't hurt her by selling out while she's alive. I'll stay until Gran is gone." Mattie shifted and raised her chin higher, and he saw the determined glint in her eyes. "You have to swear you won't tell anyone, Josh. I've never told a soul. It would kill Gran, and I won't have her hurt."

"I won't tell," he answered perfunctorily, still perplexed and mulling over her revelation. "What do you want to do?"

She looked down and ran a slender finger along the rail. Her nails were neatly trimmed, and her hands looked delicate, even though he knew she probably had as many calluses on her palms as he did.

"It may sound foolish, but for years I've dreamed of going to law school. I've read some law books." When she looked up, he saw the defiance in her bright gaze, as if she expected him to laugh at her.

Instead, he felt defeated, because she had seemed the perfect answer to his dilemma. And he felt the old guilt tug at him as he remembered how much Lisa had hated ranch life and begged him to move to the city.

"Well, there goes that idea."

"I appreciate your offer," she said, dropping her hand from the fence. "I'm flattered."

He rubbed the back of his neck. "You were the

perfect solution. I thought we'd fit together like salt and pepper.''

''I can't imagine moving here,'' she said. ''But I'm flattered.''

He gave her a faint smile and tugged on her braid. ''You underestimate yourself.''

Pleased, she smiled up at him. ''Can you take me home now?''

He nodded and started walking back toward the pickup with her. ''Are there any other relatives to take over the ranch?''

''No. Dad's only brother settled in Arizona on a ranch that belongs to his wife's family. Uncle Dan won't leave Arizona.''

''Maybe you should have discussed this with your dad.''

''It never occurred to him that I could possibly want anything else, and it hasn't occurred to Gran. And neither one would have accepted it. My sisters had a long history of rebellion from the time they were old enough to know there was some other place in the world to live.''

Josh could understand why it had never occurred to her father or grandmother that she would want to leave. Ranches all over the state had been passed down through generations of the same families. It was tradition, accepted from the time of childhood. *He* had never given a thought to doing anything else, and it hadn't occurred to him that Mattie could possibly want to leave. There was no boy in the Ryan family to pass the ranch to, and Mattie was the oldest girl. And the only one who had taken to ranching.

Disappointment washed through Josh again along

with another prickle of conscience for keeping Lisa on the ranch when she didn't want to stay. Keeping her until it killed her.

He glanced at the woman at his side, curious about her and her dreams. "Why law school?"

"I think it started when I was ten and Mom was killed by a drunk driver who had a long record of arrests. He got away without even a fine, and I was so incensed that I dreamed of growing up and becoming a lawyer and prosecuting people like that." She smiled up at him. "That was idealistic, and I was filled with childish dreams, but the idea of becoming a lawyer appeals to me. I don't want this rural existence all my life. I feel like there's more out there, and I want to have a chance to see for myself."

"What did you major in?"

"Animal science. I had a minor in English—it was what I liked the most. But I loved my Dad and would never have hurt him. He wanted me to study animal science."

"I dropped out my junior year to come home and run this place when my dad died," Josh said.

"It appears you've done a good job."

"I try. Your father could have lived to a ripe old age. If he had, what would you have done?"

"I probably would have stayed forever. Maybe at some point I would have told him what I wanted, but I doubt it. It's lonely without him, and the battles are constant—weather, sick animals—you know all the problems involved. Ranching isn't the same without him, and I don't want to fight for the ranch all my life."

They walked in silence until they reached the

pickup, and then she turned to face him. "Josh, keep looking and find a nanny. You'll be glad later. You shouldn't go into some loveless, arranged marriage."

"I want to keep Elizabeth," he said, feeling his heart constrict because he couldn't work and care for a baby at the same time.

"Let me run an ad and interview nannies. Maybe if they have to reply to me, I can help find the right one for you."

"That's a thought. I might do that. I'll write out my ad and bring it by."

She smiled, her full lips parting, a sparkle coming to her green eyes that was inviting. Why hadn't she dated? he wondered again. Just wrong men and wrong times? He contemplated what her life would be like if she left the ranch. "I think if you go to law school and become a lawyer, you'll find what you're looking for...and someone you do want to date."

She shrugged. "I'm twenty-eight and getting set in my ways."

"Come on, old lady. I'll take you home."

Relaxed, glancing at his house briefly, she climbed into the pickup and rode in comfortable silence while Josh drove her home. As he walked to the door with her, he paused and placed his hands on her shoulders. Instant awareness of his touch, of his nearness, flashed through her, and for one moment she saw clearly what she had tossed away tonight.

"If you change your mind about lawyering, let me know."

"Bring your ad over, and I'll run it and do some interviews."

"Sure, Mattie." He brushed her cheek with a kiss.

His lips were warm; there was a faint smell of beer on his breath. For a moment she wanted to lean closer, wanted to discover what it was like to kiss him. She suspected it would be best that she never know.

"Thanks for dinner, Josh. I'll never forget your proposal."

"I'm damn disappointed, Mattie. I'll be back tomorrow or the next day with my ad." He grinned and shrugged.

His lopsided grin exuded charm. Creases appeared in his cheeks; his even white teeth were a contrast to his dark skin. She could remember times in the past when she had watched him in public places and seen him laughing, looking enormously appealing. If he ever turned on the charm, she thought, it would be impossible to resist him.

She watched him stride through the darkness to his pickup and climb inside, roaring away down the road. As he drove away, loss swamped her. She looked at the land that she felt part of; the same land that sometimes made her feel suffocated. The ranch was a tough taskmaster; decisions were difficult, and the burden of running the place was squarely on her shoulders.

Darkness enveloped the ranch, and quiet settled, reminding her of how alone she was. Had she made the mistake of her life tonight? If she sold the ranch and left, would she later regret what she had done and look back on Josh's offer with longing? A loveless marriage *couldn't* be a good bargain. She thought again of Josh's fleeting kiss on her cheek. He was handsome, exciting, but she suspected that in the kind of arrangement he wanted he would barely be aware of her.

With a shrug she went inside, thankful Gran had

already gone to her own small house that was several hundred yards down the road. Right now Mattie didn't feel like answering a lot of questions about why she was home so early and why she wouldn't be going out with Josh again.

Two days later, as she stepped out of a stall in the barn, a dark silhouette filled the sunny doorway.

"Mattie?"

Her pulse jumped when she recognized Josh's bass voice. "What are you doing here?" She felt a guilty blush heat her cheeks, because his proposal had occupied most of her waking hours. Even though she had said no, she couldn't forget or get Josh out of her mind. As she watched him approach, she remembered her offer. "Did you get your ad written?"

"Irma said you were in the barn with a sick mare."

Mattie turned to rub the sorrel's neck. "She's better. Doc was here yesterday, and she's come around nicely."

Josh moved closer to look at the mare. In jeans and a white T-shirt, Josh made her aware of her own appearance, and she pushed wayward tendrils of hair from her face.

"Do you have the ad?" she repeated.

Josh turned to her, and her pulse jumped another notch as she faced him. He pushed his broad-brimmed black hat to the back of his head and thrust out his hand beside her to lean slightly against the stall while he moved closer to her. His T-shirt clung to his muscled chest and powerful biceps. Her heart began hammering as she gazed up at him. He shook his head, and she could see a look of determination in his gaze that made her mouth go dry.

"Mattie, you said you'll never sell this place as long as your grandmother is alive. Did you really mean that?"

"Yes. I won't do that to any of my family. After Irma is gone, then I'll sell," she replied, and hoped her voice didn't sound breathless. Josh was standing too close, watching her too intently. And she could tell by his stance that he was going to try to talk her into something.

"I remember your grandfather. He died some years ago."

"We lost him two years ago and Dad this year," she said stonily, momentarily feeling the sense of loss that came less often now.

"How old was your grandfather?"

"He was older than my grandmother. He was eighty-four when he died." She wanted to move away, but Josh was hemming her in. She could detect the enticing woodsy, barberry scent of his aftershave, see the faint dark stubble on his jaw. She was barely aware of their conversation, and her nerves felt as if they were jumping with little charges of electricity from his proximity.

"I remember them talking about your great-grandfather, who lived to be one hundred. How old is Irma?"

"She'll be eighty-one her next birthday."

"And how's her health?"

"She has a heart condition, but it hasn't given her trouble for several years," Mattie said. "Josh—" She paused, at a loss, disturbed by him. She tried to back up and bumped the stall. He moved closer, and she could feel the warmth of his body.

"Mattie," Josh said, his voice lowering. "I've been considering all you told me. If you're staying on the ranch as long as Irma lives, you could be here several more years," Josh said, watching her. Her eyes were wide, and the pulse near her throat was throbbing. He wondered if he disturbed her, and he found the notion refreshing. Feeling certain to his soul that she would be perfect for Elizabeth, he was willing to take some risks to get what he wanted.

Mattie's heart seemed to stop and then pound violently, because she could guess what he was getting at. "Yes, I could."

"Marry me. We'll draw up a prenuptial agreement that lets you out of the marriage when Irma dies."

"No! I can't!" Panic rose in her. She didn't know how to deal with this forceful man. She had hired and fired ranch hands, dealt with men angry with her or her father, but that had never been like this. What was it about Josh Brand that seemed to make her knees weak and her mind stop functioning?

"Listen to me," Josh ordered quietly, and she closed her mouth and then caught her lower lip with her even white teeth. "You marry me and stay for one year. Elizabeth will be a year and a half old, and by then we'll have a good nanny all settled in. You stay one year, and I'll pay for law school for you. I'll pay all your costs. I'll pay off the mortgage your dad took on the ranch."

Stunned, she stared at him while the amount of the mortgage danced in her mind.

Josh smoothed the collar of her white cotton shirt,

and Mattie drew a quick breath. How could she marry this man and live under the same roof with him? He disturbed her just standing here talking.

"If you stay five years—which would see Elizabeth into school age—I'll give you a quarter of my ranch when we part, or buy you the comparable amount or give you the money. Plus all the other."

Shocked, she blinked and bit her lip and gazed up at him in speechless amazement. "You can't! That's too much—"

"Not where my daughter is concerned," he answered quietly, but she heard the note of steel. One look into his dark eyes and she knew he meant every word he said.

"We're back to where we were. I *can't* take care of her," she said, butterflies fluttering wildly in her stomach. The man was hell-bent on getting his way.

"I know better. You run this whole damn ranch, nurse sick horses, help mares when they foal, bring calves into the world. You can hire a nanny."

"You know there's more to it than overseeing a nanny," she said, mildly annoyed and feeling a bubbling panic at his implacable tone and lavish offers. "I lost my mother when I was ten. I know what it's like to be without a mother. Your little girl *needs* a mother."

He flinched, and Mattie felt as if she had been too harsh.

"A nanny may be the best I can do," he replied stonily. "But I'll give her all the love I can. And if you're there—even for just a year—you can get us off to a good start."

"Josh, I can't—"

"Listen," he commanded in a tone that made her forget her arguments. His voice was quiet, yet there was an air of authority and determination about him that ended her talk.

"We'll draw up a prenuptial agreement. If we decide to part before Irma dies, you get your ranch back intact—and all the things I just promised you."

She closed her eyes to shut out his disturbing image. "I can't do it."

"Yes, you can. You're perfect. We can work together. You can run your ranch and I'll run mine. The difference is, you'll live at my house and be in charge of the nanny and Elizabeth. That's all."

Josh held his breath. This was the perfect woman. She would be as capable as anyone could possibly be. She was softhearted, he knew, or she never would have been as loyal to her family as she had, staying on the ranch when she dreamed of leaving. And the little he had been around her, he liked her. She hadn't talked incessantly. She could ride as well as any man he knew. She could run the ranch better than many he knew. And she was honest and forthright—refreshing qualities after the coy flirtations of the last three nannies. She was a fine-looking woman, too. Although he wouldn't have let it matter if she had been as plain as a mud hen. He wanted Mattie Ryan. He needed her. And he had to make her need him. He knew she was in tight times and shouldering the responsibility solely by herself. And he knew how lonely and frightening that could be.

She opened her eyes and looked at him. "Move away."

Instantly he stepped back, and she strode away from

him. His gaze ran over her back. Her jeans were tight, and she had an enticing little sway to her walk that made him notice her fanny and her long legs. With surprise, he realized how he was looking at her and how his body was responding—something that hadn't happened since Lisa. In spite of the flagrant enticements of the nannies, he had been as numb as the ground, but he wasn't numb now. This was a lot of woman, and a damned good-looking one at that.

Mattie spun around and faced him as if she were armed and ready to duel. She had her hands on her hips, and he could see the flash of fire in her eyes.

"I think you'll regret this terribly. Suppose you fall in love again?"

"I'm not going to. I adored Lisa and I won't fall in love. I feel numb," he said, knowing that until five minutes ago it had been the complete truth. "And I can get along out here on the ranch."

"I think you're wrong. It's too soon. In six months I think you'll feel differently and you'll want to fall in love."

"Then we can get the marriage annulled, and you can have all I promised you. Ask what you want in the prenuptial agreement. Make the stakes higher if I leave you, Mattie. Then you'll see how earnest I am about this."

Mattie stared at him while her heart raced. For the first time in her life she felt as if she might faint. She knew he was making a mistake. She was terrified at the thought of having full responsibility for a little baby. She was equally terrified at the thought of living under the same roof with a forceful, dynamic man like Josh.

At the same time she was tempted as hell to accept. She was lonely and missed working with her father. Josh was handsome, strong and masculine. She was drawn to him. The thought of living under the same roof, working with him daily, sent her heart into flurries, but it held an appeal that she could not deny. If he hadn't offered her anything, his proposal would still appeal to her. To propose marriage, even a platonic one, and add to his offer his willingness to pay the mortgage, give her a hefty settlement, pay all her law school costs—how could she turn that down?

With his dark gaze holding hers, he walked toward her. With every step he took, her heart pounded. Her palms were damp and her emotions churned.

He stopped only inches from her and tilted her chin up to gaze down into her eyes. "You're the woman I want and need. Ask what you want."

"You're more than generous with what you've offered." She could barely get out the words.

"I don't think you need time to think about it. Your grandmother lives in her own house here on the ranch, and we can move her to my ranch. You live in that house alone. How can you lose? You have everything to gain. You can walk out of the marriage at any time after the first year. I'd like you to stay at least one year. That's not asking too much, is it?"

She couldn't talk and she shook her head.

"We can go to the lawyer tomorrow. Your life will change very little."

"It'll change beyond measure if I have a baby on my hands."

"Not after we hire a nanny to look after her."

"We've been over that. You know I'd mother her if I knew how."

She stared at him, knowing he was waiting and knowing he wanted an answer right now. And she knew what she should answer to such a proposition. It would get her out of the red and into the black. It would help in so many ways. And she was so damned lonely in that empty house. Running the ranch alone was an enormous responsibility. Yet she couldn't bring herself to answer, because she kept thinking about the tiny baby he had brought over with him on that first visit. How could she take care of a baby? And if she married Josh Brand and lived under the same roof with the sexy, handsome man standing only feet from her, she would surely fall in love with him.

The notion terrified her. He already set her pulse racing. He was appealing, intelligent, dynamic. She might lose her heart completely. And he might fall in love again—with some other woman—or never love again. If she was in love with him, could she survive? And what about her dreams of law school?

"I think you know your answer," he said quietly.

"No, I don't," she replied, thoughts whirling in her mind.

"What have you got to lose?"

"Suppose I fall in love with you?" she asked bluntly. For an instant he looked startled and then he grinned with a brief appealing flash of his white teeth.

"You haven't fallen in love with anyone yet. I don't think you will, but if you do—we're married. I'll be your husband."

"You won't love me in return."

His smile vanished, and she felt as if an icy wind

swished over her as he gazed at her solemnly. "I don't think either one of us runs that risk. No, I won't love again. Not ever. But I don't think you'll fall in love with me, Mattie. You're very practical and you've made it twenty-eight years without falling in love. I don't think you will now. Whatever happens, you're getting a lot in exchange," he reminded her. "How badly do you want law school?"

"Badly enough to go the first chance I get."

"Then there's your answer. You won't fall in love if you have that goal in mind."

Josh knew what he wanted, and he suspected she was hovering on the edge of acceptance. He moved closer and saw the wary look on her face. He touched her shoulders lightly and gazed at her. He rubbed her throat with his thumb, feeling her soft, warm skin, finding her pulse. It raced, and that pleased him.

"Mattie, we can do so much for each other. Say you'll marry me. You'll gain and I'll gain and Elizabeth will gain. You won't get hurt. You can't lose."

"You said you hired three nannies and then fired them in short order. You've made three mistakes. What about me? You could regret this almost immediately."

"I'm not going to regret it."

"You don't know that!" she snapped, still flustered by his thumb running so lightly back and forth on her throat. Tingles radiated from his touch, dancing through her like tiny sparks tapping her nerves. She was disappointed by his answer, yet he was being honest. Why would he fall in love with her?

"I'll be bound for a year, as well, bound by what

I've promised you. And I told you, name what you want if I try to get out of the arrangement.''

She looked into his eyes and felt the clash of wills between them. And she was conscious of more than that. While he might be completely unaware of it, she felt an electrical tension around him. Right now she felt as if she stood too close to a raging fire. He disturbed her, and he was so handsome it was difficult to think and not just stare. Silence stretched tautly between them while she debated his offer.

As Josh watched her, he could never recall having had such a difficult time talking a woman into anything, except when he'd tried to get Lisa to stay on the ranch. And he intended to get what he wanted in this situation. He didn't see how Mattie could do anything but gain. Financially, she would be far better off. They could get along under one roof. She was biting her lip, staring at him, and he could see the turmoil in her expression. Her cheeks were flushed and her pulse raced, but he suspected she was on the verge of agreement.

''Marry me, Mattie,'' he urged again and held his breath.

They stared at each other while her heart pounded. Common sense told her the whole idea was preposterous. But his offer was as irresistible as the man himself. Taking a deep breath, closing her eyes as if she were jumping off a diving board, she nodded. ''Yes, I will.''

''Ya-hoo!'' He let out a whoop and scooped her up in his arms. Startled, she clung to him, aware of his broad shoulders beneath her arms, too conscious of being held in his embrace, a sensation that was more than pleasant. Her heart raced while he spun around.

"Josh! Put me down!"

He gave another exuberant shout and set her on her feet and hugged her. "Thank goodness!"

His arms were strong, and she felt the clean T-shirt beneath her cheek, the warmth and solid hardness of his body.

"Yahoo!" he exclaimed again and bent his head to kiss her swiftly. When his mouth touched hers, her heart thudded, and her breathing stopped. Her lips parted involuntarily. Her body seemed to contract and grow hot while her pulse roared.

Without thinking, she pushed against his chest. He stepped back, looking as startled as she felt. "We might as well kiss. We're going to marry."

"That isn't part of the deal," she mumbled, dazed, her lips still tingling.

"Whatever you want. This is great, Mattie!" His hands were on her shoulders and his dark eyes danced with excitement. "You won't regret it! I'll call a lawyer, and we'll draw up the prenuptial agreement tomorrow."

She felt her head spin. Although it had been a light, impulsive kiss, one that she was certain he had already forgotten, her lips still tingled. She felt as if lightning had streaked out of the sunny sky and zapped her. She felt hot and shaken along with being worried about his enthusiasm. "Josh, slow down."

"No, there's no need to slow down. We both know what we want. How soon can we have a wedding? Do you want a great big one?"

"No, I don't," she answered solemnly, wondering

exactly what she had let herself in for. She was un-
accustomed to impulsive, exuberant men. Her father
had been a strong, silent man of few words, and seldom had his emotions shown. How could she cope
with Josh?

"The wedding is a sham," she said, only half thinking about the ceremony, wondering more about him.
"I'm not getting all gussied up and go through all the
folderol as if it were real. And it won't look good for
you. People will think you should have waited
longer."

His smile vanished. "I adored Lisa and everyone
knows it. All right, we'll have a tiny wedding. Only
very best friends and family. How soon?"

"I have to look at a calendar."

"Let's go tell Irma."

"Don't you think we ought to go out together
maybe one more time before we announce this to the
world?"

He paused and looked at her. Mattie had her hands
on her hips again, her brow furrowed in a frown while
she bit her lip. He could see where people would gos-
sip, anyway, but it might be easier for Mattie if he
took her out a few times.

"I'll pick you up for dinner tonight. This is Tues-
day. We can go out every night this week, and Saturday we'll eat in town and everyone will see us and
start speculating about us."

"We might as well announce it's a marriage of convenience."

"No." He thought about the overtures of the nannies he had hired. And he knew Mattie had been hurt
by local men. He didn't want anyone causing her more

hurt or making fun of her marriage. And he didn't want any more women coming on to him. ''I want people to think it's real.''

She shrugged. She would prefer people thought it a genuine marriage; she'd been laughed at behind her back enough in her lifetime. ''They'll wonder why you married me.''

''Anyone with a grain of sense would be green with envy.''

''Thank you,'' she said flatly.

Josh saw the disbelief in her eyes and heard it in her voice. He guessed she had been hurt a lot of times in a lot of ways. He moved close to her and tilted up her chin to gaze down at her.

Mattie's pulse leaped as she looked at him. ''I'm not lying or flattering you to get something,'' he said quietly. ''There's no need to do either, and I'm not into lying. Do you think I would ask someone to marry me—even if it is a platonic marriage of convenience— if I didn't respect the person? I'm turning Elizabeth over to you. I wouldn't do this if I didn't like being around you. There are some women I could not abide to have under my roof. We're going to be living together and working together. I have to have someone intelligent, capable—and someone I like, Mattie.''

She stared at him, her heart thudding, while his words wrapped around her like a silken cloak. And she knew with a sinking feeling that she was going to fall in love with this man who would not love her in return and who would someday dissolve their marriage without a backward glance. She wanted a law degree, she reminded herself, and she had better keep that in mind and hang on to it like a lifeline or she was in for the worst hurt of her life.

Four

"**Y**ou look gorgeous, love!" Standing in the church's bridal room, Irma smiled up at Mattie, her blue eyes sparkling, while her bifocals slipped down her nose. When Mattie shivered, Irma touched her arms with shaky fingers. "Child, you're ice-cold!"

"I don't think I should have had this big wedding." Mattie wanted to cry out the truth—that the man she was marrying needed a nanny and not a wife—but she and Josh had agreed to keep the truth to themselves. She knew it would hurt Irma to hear why they were going through with this ceremony.

"Nonsense!"

"Grandma, he's only been widowed a little over four months now." ·

"Don't be so old-fashioned, Mattie!" Irma sniffed, touching the lace on Mattie's white silk wedding gown. "You're both from old families, and we have so many relatives and friends. Why, your uncle Dan flew his whole family from Arizona for this wedding. If your father can't give your hand in marriage, at least his brother graciously offered. So, see, it would be ridiculous for you to slip off and have a tiny wedding. We might as well celebrate and have a party. You won't be doing this again in your lifetime."

"You're right about that," Mattie mumbled, looking over her grandmother's head at her reflection in the oval mirror. Her hair was in an elaborate pile with curling tendrils tumbling down her neck. She barely recognized herself, yet she was pleased with the image in the mirror. Her insides fluttered and she wished she had insisted on a small wedding, but Irma had had her heart set on giving her this wedding and inviting all her friends and their relatives. Sunlight streamed through the window, and as Mattie adjusted the veil behind her head, her diamond engagement ring flashed with brilliance.

With a knock on the door, Andrea thrust her head into the room. "Wow, look at you!" she cried, stepping inside and closing the door behind her.

Mattie had asked Carlina to be her matron of honor and Andrea, her younger sister, to be maid of honor. Andrea crossed the room in a deep blue knee-length dress that Mattie had selected. It was practical, and Mattie wished again that she had insisted Irma give up the idea of a large wedding. Yet as she looked into Irma's twinkling eyes, she knew she wouldn't have had the heart to hurt her grandmother.

When Andrea stood beside her, Mattie looked at her younger sister in the mirror. "You look so pretty,"

Mattie said. Andrea was petite, with blond curly hair and deep blue eyes. Both her sisters were under five foot six. Next to Andrea and Carlina, Mattie always felt too tall.

"You're a beautiful bride, Mattie. I'm so happy for you!"

When they turned to hug, a knot burned in Mattie's throat. She had been closest to Andrea, and had always felt like a mother to her baby sister. While Mattie longed to tell Andrea that it was a sham marriage, she couldn't. If Andrea knew how this marriage was a loveless contract of convenience that would pay her college tuition and bills, she would be crushed and beg Mattie not to wed.

"Hi," came a lilting greeting as Carlina swept into the small bridal room. A pretty brunette with blue eyes, accentuated by the blue dress, Carlina crossed the room. "You look gorgeous!" she said, hugging Mattie.

"You're both great to come for the wedding."

"I can't believe this whirlwind courtship, and that you're marrying Josh Brand!" Carlina exclaimed. "I always thought you'd marry someone quiet and solitary like Dad."

"How would you know what Josh is like?" Mattie asked, barely giving thought to her question.

"Remember, I dated one of his friends for a time. Speaking of time, they're waiting for the bride. Uncle Dan is ready. Grandmother, they're looking for you."

"My dear, if only your precious mother and father could see you," Irma said, her blue eyes filling with tears.

Mattie hugged her, and soon her sisters left with

their grandmother. Mattie took one last look at herself in the mirror. "What am I doing?" she whispered, feeling a sudden urge to run out the back door. Remembering the bills that Josh had promised to pay, she took a deep breath, squared her shoulders and left to find her uncle.

Looking like a smaller version of her father, her uncle stood waiting. As she joined him in the narthex, she felt another lump in her throat. With a thick head of graying hair and a square jaw, his blue eyes flicked over her and he smiled. "You look beautiful," he whispered when he linked her arm through his.

"Thank you," she replied, barely aware of what she was saying, an inner voice screaming that she was acting out a farce. The church was filled with friends. Irma had been seated in a front pew. Across the aisle from her sat Sibyl and Thornton Bridges, Josh's mother and stepfather. Mattie knew Elizabeth was in her grandmother's lap because Josh had decided he wanted his daughter at the wedding.

As soon as Carlina and Andrea reached the end of the aisle, a peal of organ music heralded the bride, and the guests stood. Mattie moved down the aisle, her gaze meeting the dark eyes of her husband-to-be. She tingled from head to toe. He looked dark, dangerous, sexy. He was everything in a man that she knew nothing about, or how to deal with. The dates she had had with him had been uneasy evenings; she felt he'd been barely aware of her existence. And now with this brief ceremony, all the Ryan land would belong to him as well as to her. He was a threat and at the same time, a salvation. And his steady gaze made her pulse race, her palms damp and her breathing irregular.

Feeling a leaden weight momentarily lift from his shoulders, Josh inhaled. While he congratulated himself that his nanny problems were over, he stared in surprise. The woman drifting down the aisle toward him was beautiful. He had realized Mattie was attractive, but he could not recall ever seeing her in a dress until now. The golden-haired woman gazing steadily at him was gorgeous. His gaze flicked over her, pausing momentarily at the heart-shaped neckline of the white dress and the alluring curves it revealed. Her waist was tiny and she had a regal bearing as she came down the aisle. He felt better. She was intelligent, beautiful, cooperative. He had made a lot of deals—buying land, buying horses and cattle—but this might be the best deal he had ever made. Mattie stopped a few feet from him, and her green-eyed gaze never left his. The men in this county must have been blind and just plain stupid to let Mattie slip past them, but thank heavens they had.

Staring at her husband-to-be, Mattie didn't hear the words being said, and then Uncle Dan placed her hand in Josh's warm grip. She brushed her uncle's cheek with a kiss before turning to Josh. His dark eyes were unfathomable. She could barely repeat her vows, whispering, "I, Matilda Maude Ryan, take thee, Joshua Kirby Brand, to be my lawful wedded husband."

It was impossible, yet she was repeating vows and then listening as Josh's bass voice clearly responded, "...to have and to hold from this day forward..."

Dazed, she went through the ceremony. Looking at the wide gold band Josh had placed on her finger and the plain gold band she had slipped on his, Mattie felt as if she were in a dream. Her breath caught when the minister intoned, "You may kiss the bride."

She looked into dark brown eyes that held a glint of sadness and she realized he was remembering his wife. His *real* wife. He leaned down and brushed her lips with the most feathery touch of his mouth, yet it sent a wave of warmth curling through her down to her toes. As they looked at each other, the sadness in his expression vanished, momentarily replaced by an intense look that seemed to probe her soul. This time his eyes were filled with curiosity.

And then the moment was gone. He linked her arm through his and guided her down the aisle. He paused to brush his mother's cheek with a kiss before swinging Elizabeth up into his arms, flashing a smile at Mattie that caused a sting of wistful longing. If only this was a real wedding and his smile was one of true love!

Raising her chin, she told herself to forget such silly notions. She had a business arrangement with the man and nothing more. The moment they emerged into the narthex, her attention was taken up by well-wishers.

As soon as pictures were taken—something Irma had arranged—they drove to Mattie's ranch for the reception that spread through the house and across the patio. Inside and out, tables were laden with food. The chocolate groom's cake was in the house; the immense white wedding cake was on a table on the patio. Also on the patio, fiddlers played country tunes. Within minutes, Josh was standing in front of Mattie. He had shed his coat and tie, rolled back his sleeves, and the sight of him made her pulse skitter.

"Shall we dance? Everyone's waiting for us to do the first two-step."

"I don't know how to dance!" she said, horrified that she hadn't thought ahead to this moment.

He grinned, amusement flickering in his dark eyes. "Relax. A two-step is the simplest there is. Just walk backward and step in time to the music. One step and two."

"I can't!" she exclaimed, aware of people gathering to watch them.

"C'mon, Mattie. This is easier than barrel racing, and I know how well you do that."

His arm circled her waist, and he held her hand as he pushed her back. She began to move, raising her chin, her heart fluttering. Her feet bumped his and she felt clumsy and embarrassed, wanting to pull away. His hand tightened on her waist.

"Relax," he said softly. "Step back, step together, step back," he said calmly, and her panic diminished. She caught on to his step and moved with him. His dark gaze held hers, amusement still dancing in his eyes. All her concern vanished. She became aware of Josh holding her, their bodies moving together, their legs brushing. Wind tugged at her hair and the April sunshine was hot on her shoulders while she whirled around the patio in his arms. As his expression became solemn, her pulse jumped. An electric tension strummed across her nerves. She was aware of every inch of contact with him, his arm pressing so lightly on her waist, guiding her, his hand holding hers firmly.

When his gaze lowered to her mouth, her racing heartbeat jumped again. She was responding in an elemental way to him, a dangerous way, because he didn't care about her. This man was her husband now. Even if this was a sham marriage, their lives would be intimately bound. He would never fall in love with her and she should remember the risks.

The music ended, another tune commenced and other couples began to dance.

He dropped his hands to his side. "They're motioning to us to come cut the cake."

She nodded and walked with him to the table with the fancy cake that was decorated with roses of pale pink icing, delicate live rosebuds and lacy green fern. After they dutifully cut the cake, friends pressed in with best wishes, and she was separated from him.

"Mattie, you are the most beautiful bride!"

Mattie turned as Sibyl Bridges, Josh's mother, hugged her and stepped back. Feeling tall and awkward, Mattie looked down at Mrs. Bridges whose blue eyes sparkled. "I couldn't believe it when Josh called to tell me that he was marrying you, but now I am so thankful. He already looks much happier."

"I hope so," Mattie said, wishing she could tell Sibyl Bridges the truth. The pretty brunette didn't have a gray hair in her head and she looked too young to be Josh's mother, but Mattie had known her all the years she was growing up, and she knew Sibyl was older than she appeared.

"Be patient with him, Mattie. At least I can sleep nights now, knowing that he's in good hands and my prayers have been answered. I've known you since the day you were born, and I couldn't be happier."

Guilt plagued Mattie as she smiled at Sibyl. Hating the deception, Mattie felt at a loss for words, dimly wondering about the Brands and all this faith they had in her. It would have been reassuring years earlier if

she had known someone besides her family felt that
way about her.

"Mattie, Mrs. Bridges, come here for a picture,"
Carlina called, and the conversation ended.

An hour later Mattie stood in a group with her sisters and their friends. Glancing beyond them, she
watched the dancers, remembering the moments in
Josh's arms. Someone said her name and she turned
to see Carlina motioning to her. "It's time to toss your
bouquet and your garter."

She had argued briefly about the two customs with
her sisters, but had given up, deciding it was impossible to tell them why she didn't want to do anything
traditional.

Andrea and single female friends lined up and she
threw the bouquet over her shoulder, sending it flying
through the air while the hopefuls squealed with eagerness.

She looked up to find Josh standing before her.
Once again, amusement flashed in his dark eyes. "I
believe I'm supposed to remove your garter and give
it a toss for the single guys."

She could feel the blush that burned her face as she
cautiously pulled up her wedding dress.

Josh saw the pink flush that flooded her cheeks.
Mattie was a surprising collection of contradictions.
She was embarrassed for him to see her leg, yet he
suspected she was quite competent at castrating a calf
or delivering a colt or any other task that would make
most of the women in the room faint.

He knelt and looked at a long, shapely leg clad in
a sheer silken stocking. He slid down the garter, his
knuckles brushing her leg. She placed her hand on his

shoulder as she raised her foot. Holding her slender ankle, he slipped the garter over her foot, his fingers lightly stroking her ankle. The woman had gorgeous legs. He stood then, watching her, and when she stared back at him, her green eyes were enormous. He felt ensnared, held by an invisible current that startled him. Giving his shoulders a shake, he tossed the garter over his shoulder and heard the laughter and shouts of the men behind him.

"I've seen women's legs before, Mattie," he said lightly.

"Not mine," she remarked, then she turned and was gone with a switch of her hips.

Startled, Josh watched her and chuckled softly under his breath. For what might be the hundredth time, he couldn't imagine why some man hadn't noticed her and claimed her already.

It was another hour before Mattie had a moment to herself. Leaving the sunny patio, she stepped into the cool hall. People clustered in the living room, and she glanced into the dining room. Josh stood alone at the serving table. He downed a glass of champagne as if it had been Scotch, and for an instant he closed his eyes with his jaw grimly set.

She realized he hurt and that the sounds of music, and people talking, had all become jarring and discordant. Even though this marriage was necessary for both of them, she suspected he hated it, and she was not pleased about it, either. Impulsively she stepped into the room, going to his side to touch his arm lightly.

"Can we go now?"

He looked down at her with red eyes. He wiped at them quickly, but she saw his tears. A muscle worked in his jaw, and she knew he didn't want her at his side. Stung, she clamped her lips closed. This had been his idea, not hers.

"I'll get Elizabeth and tell Mom and Thornton goodbye," he replied. "Say your goodbyes and let's get the hell out. My trailer is in your garage."

She nodded and hurried to find her grandmother. In minutes she met him in the kitchen. He held Elizabeth and a bulging bag.

"Sure you want to leave without any fanfare?" he asked.

"Yes," she answered emphatically, exhausted by going through motions that held no meaning.

"Are you leaving now?" Lottie asked, studying them. She dried her hands, then smoothed them on the white apron tied over her crisp black uniform.

"Yes, Lottie," Mattie said, turning to hug the woman who had been like a mother to her for years. "I've told Gran and my sisters goodbye. It was a wonderful wedding. Thank you for all you did. I'll call home soon."

"You take care of yourself and your new family." Lottie released her and wiped her eyes. Josh held the door, and then they rushed across the yard to the garage, where the shiny truck and horse trailer waited. Josh fastened Elizabeth into her car seat and gave her a bag of toys. "Here, sweetie. We're going for a trip."

She laughed and pulled out a board, poking a picture of a cow. As the sound of moos filled the truck, he grinned. "Hope you don't mind noise. She likes all the gadgets that squeak and rumble and play tunes."

"Of course I don't mind," Mattie said, trying to fold her wedding dress around her legs. "I should have changed, but then everyone would have made such a fuss." Josh tucked her dress around her and closed the door.

He walked to the driver's side, then slid behind the wheel. "I think they realize we're leaving," he said, turning on the engine and pulling out of the garage. People had spilled out the kitchen door and were waving and calling to them. Josh waved in return, pressed the accelerator, and they sped down the drive.

"We're off for a weekend in Fort Worth. You can get acquainted with Elizabeth and we'll buy some new horses."

"Don't forget—tomorrow at the hotel I have interviews with prospective nannies," Mattie reminded him, wondering if she had packed a copy of the ad she'd placed in the Dallas and Fort Worth papers.

When he didn't answer her, she glanced at him. His jaw was set, a muscle working, and she felt a pang of sympathy for him. "This has been a bad day for you, hasn't it? You're remembering."

His gaze met hers directly and he nodded. "Sorry. No reflection on you. The wedding brought back memories. I loved my wife very much," he added tersely. "I miss her."

Feeling like an unwanted intruder in his life, Mattie nodded and twisted around to look at Elizabeth who was turning dials and listening to barks and meows. Every time she looked at Elizabeth, Mattie felt uncertain. She knew nothing about babies, yet Elizabeth seemed cheerful and happy to amuse herself. Mattie remembered how close she had been to her father and wondered if Elizabeth would have the same bond with Josh. He seemed to adore his daughter, so she imagined the two would be close.

Mattie glanced at her husband again. His profile was to her as he drove; his hands looked strong and competent on the wheel. Had she traded her independence foolishly? she wondered with a start. Then she reminded herself once again of all she was gaining and finally settled in the seat to ride quietly until they reached their destination.

It was dusk by the time they arrived in Fort Worth. Lights twinkled over the downtown area, giving a feeling of celebration, yet Mattie's apprehension grew as they swept up to the front door of the big hotel.

"I feel incredibly conspicuous in this wedding dress."

Josh grinned and leaned across the seat. "Relax. Who do you know here? No one."

"True," she replied as a valet opened the door for her and she stepped out of the truck.

Shrugging into his coat, Josh unbuckled Elizabeth, made arrangements for the car and luggage and then followed Mattie into the hotel. She swept inside as if she owned the place, and he bit back a smile when he handed Elizabeth to her and set the carrier on the floor.

"I'll check in. Everyone watching will think we had Elizabeth out of wedlock," he said with a wink.

Consternation filled her. Realizing he was right, Mattie stared at his broad shoulders as he crossed the room. He had pulled on his coat again, and it swung slightly with each step he took. She lifted her chin and smiled at Elizabeth, refusing to look around, deciding she did not care what anyone thought.

"You're a good traveler," she said, smoothing Elizabeth's beautiful pale pink dress. The pink bow that had been in her wispy hair during the wedding ceremony had long ago disappeared. Elizabeth smiled, her one lower tooth showing while she made cooing sounds at Mattie. Her heart warmed to the child.

In seconds Josh was back at her side, taking Elizabeth from her, his hands brushing her arm lightly. "They'll bring the bags."

She followed in silence as they crossed the lobby and entered an elevator. Josh had rented a suite with two bedrooms on the top floor. When she stepped inside the spacious suite, she was aware she was alone with her new husband and his baby. Moments later, he handed Elizabeth to her while he opened the door for the bellhop. Mattie crossed the room to show Elizabeth the view that was filled with the sparkling lights of Fort Worth. Behind her she heard Josh close the door behind the bellhop and pick up the phone.

"I've ordered dinner to be sent up here. I thought it would be easier because of Elizabeth, but if you'd rather—"

"Dinner here is fine," she answered.

"I can order champagne, Mattie, but would you rather have wine?"

"I'd rather have a bottle of bourbon," she answered flatly and then noticed the twitch of his lips. "Get whatever you want. I used to have a drink in the evenings with Dad."

"Bourbon sounds good to me," Josh replied and talked to someone on the phone. As soon as he replaced the receiver, he picked up her bags. "I requested a bed for Elizabeth, so one room should have a baby bed. We can move it if you want. You take the room of your choice."

"Don't move the baby bed. Either room is fine with me."

"In a few more minutes, she'll be screeching for her bottle. I'll unpack her formula and get it fixed." He motioned toward an open door. "Let's see who gets which room."

Mattie followed him into a luxurious bedroom with a king-size bed. "I could get lost in here," she said without thinking, looking at the white and beige decor. Sliding glass doors opened onto a balcony.

"This is your room then. Here is your luggage. I'll take Li'l Bit." He held out his arms to Elizabeth who wriggled and went to him eagerly. His gaze drifted down over Mattie. "She's wrinkled your dress."

Mattie smiled at him. "I won't be wearing it again."

He stroked her throat lightly with warm fingers as his expression became solemn. "You were a beautiful bride, Mattie."

"Thank you." Her heart missed a beat as she gazed up at him.

"You deserve a hell of a lot more than you're getting."

"I agreed to our bargain. I think you're being very generous."

"I wasn't talking about land or money," he said gruffly, his gaze dropping to her mouth and then sliding lower for only a moment. His lashes were dark against his cheeks, and beneath his scrutiny her pulse raced.

Elizabeth began to fuss and he moved away. "I'll feed you now, Li'l Bit. You've been a good girl today," he said, talking softly to his daughter as he left the room and closed the door behind him.

Mattie stood rooted to the spot, his words whirling in her mind. He thought she was beautiful. The idea washed over her with more warmth than Texas summer sunshine.

Mattie returned to the window to stare below at the twinkling lights. She felt alone, yet images of the day—memories and moments—comforted her. Elizabeth began to cry and Mattie glanced at the closed door to the adjoining bedroom. As the squalls grew louder, she wondered whether she should offer her help. She crossed the room to knock on the door. "Josh?"

"Come in."

"Do you need help?" she asked, opening the door to a bedroom even larger than hers. Mirrors covered one wall, floor-to-ceiling glass covered another. Elizabeth was in the middle of the big bed, screaming and kicking.

"I'm trying to get her formula poured. If you'll just hold her—"

Mattie picked up the child, jiggling her. Momentarily Elizabeth's screams died to low sobs. "Dada," she said, holding out her arms to Josh and wriggling.

Singing softly to Elizabeth, Mattie patted her and went to stand beside him to watch him mix the formula, glancing briefly at him as he concentrated on pouring from a can. Elizabeth quieted and Mattie smoothed her hair. "That's a sweetie," she said softly, thinking how warm and soft and cuddly Elizabeth was.

When Josh finished mixing the formula, he capped up a bottle. "Now I can take her," he said, lifting Elizabeth from her arms. Tiny hands grabbed the bottle and Elizabeth settled in his embrace, her fingers playing over the bottle while he held it for her.

Mattie was still in her high-heeled pumps, yet she still had to look up at Josh. It was such an unusual occurrence that she spoke without thinking. "How tall are you?"

"Six foot six," he answered, grinning. "You're a nice height, Mattie."

"Sure. With only a few exceptions, we were the two tallest people at our wedding." She glanced at Elizabeth. "Looks like she's happy," Mattie said, and turned as they heard a knock at the door.

"That's probably the bellhop with our bourbon. Get my billfold out of my hip pocket and tip him."

Blushing, aware of her fingers brushing against his backside, she withdrew his billfold, opened it and took money out. She answered the door, and motioned where the bellhop should set the cart with its glasses, bottle of bourbon, bottles of soda and bucket of ice.

She returned to Josh's room to place his billfold on a table. He was seated, holding Elizabeth, talking softly to her, his long legs stretched out before him.

Mattie left without a word, aware of his dark gaze on her as she closed the door behind her.

Drawn again to the panoramic view, she went to the window. Directly beneath were the twinkling lights of downtown. Across the city additional lights sparkled, and she stood gazing at the view, remembering the wedding that now seemed like a dream. The western horizon was still a pink glow, but the sky overhead was indigo.

What would the future hold? Mattie wondered. Could she live with this dynamic man and take care of the tiny little person that was Elizabeth? She would have a nanny and a cook to help her, but she knew she would become involved with Elizabeth. Would she be able to give Elizabeth the love and support she needed?

Mattie turned away and looked at herself in the mirror, knowing it would be the last time she would see herself in a wedding dress.

She unfastened the bustled train and let it fall, then carefully removed the cap and veil and slowly took down her hair. She intended to braid her hair and change to jeans—to settle back into the life she knew as much as she could—but her hands moved slowly while she shut her mind to thoughts of a real wedding night. When her hair was finally unpinned, she shook her head, the golden mane swirling across her shoulders, then she reached back to unfasten the long row of buttons.

It was an effort, but she refused to ask Josh for help. Finally, after many contortions, she had the last difficult button undone. When she stepped out of the dress, it fell around her with a swish, cool air fanning softly across her ankles. She wore a white silk teddy, a ridiculous undergarment, she realized now, that she had bought on a whim.

A loud cry from the next room made her turn. Since arriving in Fort Worth, the baby's normally sunny disposition had vanished. Tossing the wedding gown on the bed and kicking off the high heels, Mattie opened her suitcase.

She unpacked, placing her clothes in a drawer. The loud cries hadn't diminished, and she paused, frowning as she glanced over her shoulder. What was bothering Elizabeth?

"Mattie!"

Josh's call was full of alarm. Grabbing up a shirt, she was about to yank it on, then looked down at her bare legs and tossed it aside. "I'm coming!" She stepped back into the wedding dress instead, yanked it up and slithered into the tiny cap sleeves, holding the gaping back closed as she dashed into the next room.

Five

"Can you help? I don't know what's wrong."

Looking distraught, Josh was pulling off Elizabeth's baby T-shirt. "All that formula came back up," he said. He was bare chested, and wet splotches showed on the leg of his dark tux pants. Elizabeth's pink dress was already in a heap on the bed, and his white shirt was tossed over a chair. "I should have changed her before I fed her. Can you get a wet cloth?"

For just an instant while she looked at the rippling muscles in his back, Mattie was immobile and felt something clench deep inside her. Then she realized what he had asked and she hurried to the bathroom, releasing the back of her dress to dampen and wring out the washcloth. She returned and handed it to him.

"She acts like she wants her bottle again. I'm going to fix her a little juice. Can you take her? I've changed her."

Mattie took the squirming, crying Elizabeth who was clad only in a diaper. Mattie washed her face gently and then picked her up, and walked around, momentarily forgetting her dress was unfastened.

"Here, can you put this on her?" Josh handed a tiny cotton shirt to Mattie and she laid Elizabeth on the bed to slip the shirt on her. She picked the baby up again and jiggled her slightly as she walked around. Elizabeth quieted and snuggled down against Mattie's shoulder.

Uncertain what had caused Elizabeth's upset, Josh poured a small amount of apple juice into a bottle. He glanced around, then paused, his eyes narrowing as he looked at Mattie. Elizabeth's head was on her shoulder and his baby was quiet. His fears diminished for the child and instead his attention shifted to the woman.

Mattie walked across the room, talking softly to Elizabeth and jiggling her slightly with each step, and he knew Mattie must have forgotten about her unbuttoned state. His gaze drifted down her back that was covered only by a silken teddy. The wedding dress covered her bottom and legs, but what he could see of the small of her back was tantalizing. Her hair was down, swinging slightly with each step, hiding much of her back.

She turned around, her gaze meeting his. "Elizabeth is quieting down."

For the first time he really looked at Mattie with her hair down. She took his breath away. Her long hair was a golden cascade, tumbling over her bare shoulders, a tempting cloud a man would like to sink his fingers into. By holding Elizabeth tightly against her, Mattie anchored her dress, but it had slipped low enough to give him an enticing view of the creamy skin of her shoulders.

He had spent the day fighting painful memories of his joyous first wedding. The past twenty-four hours had bound him in grief that tore at his emotions. Now Mattie looked feminine and enticing, radiating a healthy vitality that was like a lifeline in a storm. Longing struck him, a hungry need to feel her softness, to drown himself in passion.

With an effort he shifted his attention back to Elizabeth. Setting down the bottle, he crossed the room and took Elizabeth from Mattie. The child snuggled against him, closed her eyes and placed her thumb in her mouth. He carried her to her bed and gently lowered her. He touched her forehead. "She's warm from crying, but I don't think she has a fever. What do you think?"

"I don't think I'd know," Mattie answered, but she walked to the bed and leaned over the railing to touch Elizabeth's forehead. The baby's eyes were closed, and she was breathing deeply. "I don't think she has a fever. She feels hot and damp. If she had fever, I'd think she would feel dry."

He straightened and turned to face Mattie. "Thanks for coming to the rescue. That doesn't happen often."

He stood only inches away and he was bare chested. She couldn't resist. Her gaze lowered, examining his smooth skin stretched over powerful muscles, his broad chest that tapered to a flat stomach. She yanked her gaze back up to meet his and became aware of her own disheveled appearance.

Watching her, he reached out, his hands catching her dress and pulling it slightly up on her arms.

Her pulse skittered as she stared back at him, aware of his knuckles brushing her arms. "I was changing clothes when you called," she said, feeling heat rise in her cheeks as she reached behind her to gather the back of her dress in her hand.

His gaze lowered, sliding down to her mouth, and her lips tingled as if he had touched her with his fingers instead of merely looking at her. His gaze slipped lower. "You're being cheated, Mattie."

"I knew what I was doing and I had a choice. I'm gaining from our bargain," she answered, wishing she didn't sound breathless, and hoping he couldn't detect her racing pulse.

Her green eyes were enormous as she stared at him. With the mass of golden hair, she was more beautiful than ever. She was trying to gather her dress together in back, blushing as he studied her. "I better go," she said abruptly and hurried out of the room.

Reluctantly Josh watched her go, guilt plaguing him. He had locked her in a marriage that would keep other men away from her now. Even if Mattie had kept them away through her own choice in the past, he still felt guilty. She was beautiful, intelligent, capable. She should be dating, finding a life and future for herself with someone who could give her children and a family. She should no more be married to him than she should be wasting away alone on that ranch of hers.

He shook his head, reminding himself that it was none of his business if she had always preferred to stay alone on her ranch. She was an intelligent adult who had accepted his bargain quite willingly. Pushing his wayward thoughts aside, he crossed the room to unpack his bags.

In her room Mattie unpacked, changed to jeans and a T-shirt, braided her hair, slipped her feet into worn moccasins and went into the living area. Standing beside the cart with the drinks, Josh turned, his gaze flicking over her impersonally as he held up the bottle of bourbon.

"What'll you have? Soda?"

"A double, no ice."

He glanced at her again with curiosity in his eyes. "The day that bad?"

She shook her head. "Not really. We have a good bargain." He wore jeans and a T-shirt and his snakeskin boots. His black hair was no longer tied behind his head, but hung in a shaggy cut just below his collar. There was an air of wildness about him even when he was doing nothing except standing in a hotel room in a big city. He looked as if he belonged on the back of a stallion, fighting the elements. Was it his dark looks and Kiowa blood that gave him that touch of wildness?

He handed her a glass and picked up a drink that looked as strong as hers, only his had ice. He held up his glass in a toast. "Here's to a happy, successful bargain, Mattie."

She touched his glass, gazing into his eyes while she drank the entire contents and set down the glass. Her pulse fluttered beneath his probing gaze.

"Dinner's on its way. We can eat in here or out on the balcony. The night has probably cooled a few degrees."

"Let's eat outside."

He offered her another drink, but she shook her head. "Only one."

On the balcony he pulled a chair near hers, sat down and propped his feet on the brick wall while they talked about the scheduled interviews for the nanny position.

When dinner arrived, they ate their steaks and continued talking long into the night.

"I've never traveled out of Texas," Mattie said. "I used to think Fort Worth was the largest city in the world when Dad would bring me here as a child."

Startled, Josh studied her. "You haven't traveled anywhere else?"

"No. I stayed in Texas for college. One time we drove over the border, but two hours in Mexico hardly counts for out-of-state travel."

"Your dad should have let you go."

Mattie glanced at him, surprised at the fierceness in his voice. "You sound as if someone held you here, too."

"No. I'm the one who held someone. Lisa, my wife, didn't like living on the ranch. She loved cities and people. She always wanted to get away, wanted me to move to town. After she was pregnant, it became a real issue. She was an interior decorator from Houston. She wanted to move back to Houston. I should have done what she wanted," he said, running his fingers across his eyes.

"Did you two discuss it before you married?"

He slanted a look at Mattie, and she felt foolish for her question.

"Hellfire, we didn't discuss anything. I was wildly in love. I feel like I killed her, keeping her on the ranch."

"That's dreadful!" Mattie stared at him, horrified

he would feel so guilty. "Didn't she have a car wreck?"

"Yes, it was a flash flood that swept her car off an old bridge on our place. She was on her way to Dallas to shop. Thank heaven she left Li'l Bit home with me. If I had moved to the city or let her go like she wanted—"

He broke off, and Mattie impulsively reached out to squeeze his arm, feeling the hard muscle beneath her fingers. "You couldn't foresee that. Your life is that ranch as much as my father's was. Or mine now, I guess. You shouldn't blame yourself."

He turned to look at her, took her hand in his and spread her fingers against his other palm, running his fingers over hers. She tingled from the touch as she watched him, still caught in his dark, unfathomable gaze.

"You're nice, Mattie," he said, his voice losing its gruffness. "This is a hell of a wedding night for you."

"It's good," she said, removing her hand. "My debts are paid, my tuition will be paid. Last month this time I was sitting home alone at night, worrying about Dad's debts. This is much better. Actually, you're the one who is having a hell of a wedding night," she said quietly, knowing he was hurting.

"No, and I mean that. Today was bad, but tonight's been much better. You and I didn't have great expectations about tonight," he added lightly. They both sat in silence while she thought about their bargain and their future.

"Josh, I've been thinking about law school. I'd like to go ahead and apply and see if I can get accepted. I'll have to study for the entrance exam."

"Sure. Go ahead."

"As soon as we get a nanny situated, I'll be able to spend some time studying."

Mattie enjoyed his company. It was pleasant on the balcony with sounds of the city quieting as the hour grew later. A couple of times Josh checked on Elizabeth, then returned to sit quietly and talk some more.

Knowing the hour was growing late, yet hating to see the evening end, Mattie glanced at his watch. "What time is it? It must be two o'clock in the morning."

"How about almost four o'clock?" he asked with amusement in his voice as he looked at his watch.

Startled, she glanced at him. He reached out a long arm, winding her braid in his hand and tugging lightly. "You're good company, Mattie. You should have gotten out and met men and had a real life."

"I had a real life," she said. "It's easier to relax with you. I don't do well in the dating scene."

"Bull. I'll bet some men turned green with envy when you walked down the aisle today."

"Bull is right," she said dryly, giving a jerk of her head to free her braid. She abruptly stood.

He came up beside her, so close that her pulse jumped. Breezes tugged lightly at her hair and she caught the scent of his masculine cologne. He placed his hands on her shoulders and she could feel the warmth of his palms through the thin T-shirt.

"When you go to law school, Mattie, let men take you out. I have the feeling you've been saying no so long, you don't know how to say yes."

"I said yes to you."

"That doesn't involve your emotions, your body or

your heart. It's a bargain that's as much business as buying cattle. Besides, I pushed you a little.''

Mattie was annoyed. ''Whether you realize it or not, we've bound our lives closely together. But I'll remember your advice to say yes to men when I'm in law school,'' she snapped, then brushed past him, hurrying to her room to close the door. She felt flustered, bothered by him. Up to now she had really enjoyed the evening and his companionship. She paused to stare at her reflection in the mirror. ''Don't fall in love with him,'' she warned her image. ''He won't love you back.''

She changed to the red cotton nightshirt she always wore, slipped into bed and was asleep in minutes. It seemed she had just closed her eyes when loud cries erupted from the next room. She groaned, rolling over and pulling the pillow over her head, but she could still hear Elizabeth. When the crying continued incessantly, she tossed aside the pillow and sat up in bed, wondering what was happening.

''Mattie? Mattie, can you come in here?''

Josh's voice wasn't as loud as when he had called for help before, but loud enough. With another groan she swung her feet to the floor and rushed to his room.

''What's wrong?'' she asked, opening the door.

He stood in the middle of the room holding Elizabeth and wearing jeans that were unbuttoned at the waist, riding low on his slender hips. Elizabeth was sobbing and wriggling in his arms.

''She doesn't want her bottle, and I don't know what's wrong.''

Feeling helpless, Mattie crossed the room. ''If you don't know, I surely don't!''

He thrust Elizabeth into her arms, and Mattie began walking and talking softly to the crying child. "Where's her bottle? Maybe she'll drink it now."

He handed the bottle to her, and she turned Elizabeth in her arms, holding out the bottle. With a screech Elizabeth shoved it away and Mattie felt uncertain. "Josh, I don't know what's wrong. I don't know one thing about babies."

"I don't know much, either," he said. Suspecting Josh was desperate for her to try to do something, she began to walk back and forth, singing softly. Elizabeth was hot and damp, her ringlets plastered to her head, her face red from crying. Mattie placed her against her shoulder and jiggled her, patting her on the back and singing to her. She smoothed the tiny cotton nightshirt that clung damply to the child. In seconds, Elizabeth cuddled on her shoulder, hiccupped and became quiet. Mattie felt a rush of satisfaction.

As soon as Elizabeth quieted, Josh relaxed. He rubbed his neck. "She hasn't been this way except once before when she got her tooth."

"Maybe she's getting more teeth. Have you looked?"

"No, and we're not going to now. You're doing great with her," he said, thankful Elizabeth had stopped fussing. "They may throw us out of the hotel. My tiny little daughter has a voice that can bring down the roof."

"That she does," Mattie said.

He watched Mattie cross the room. Now that his fears had calmed over Elizabeth, he became aware of Mattie. His gaze drifted down over her long hair, the nightshirt, her long bare legs. She turned to walk across the room and he was mesmerized. She had gorgeous, shapely long legs that had always been hidden by jeans—or today, by her wedding dress. He felt his body tighten and his gaze raked over her again. She was preoccupied with Elizabeth, ignoring him, and he was astounded by his response to the sight of her.

He had been numb to women, devastated by his loss. He thought about the nannies who had come on to him, flirting, wearing enticing sheer nightgowns and bikinis. He had felt nothing with any of them.

Now here was Mattie in a faded cotton nightshirt that looked as if it had belonged to her father. She didn't flirt; she wasn't interested in romance. She didn't have a coy bone in her body, yet the sight of her in the shirt was turning him on like neon.

The nightshirt hit her midthigh, but from there down the view was fantastic. And he realized he was coming back to life at a time he didn't want to, and for a woman who was a business partner and nothing more. Her future included law school, not ranching. And she had sworn she knew nothing about men, so she wouldn't be interested in fooling around.

Unable to stop looking at her sexy legs, he studied her. Was she as innocent as she sometimes indicated by her blushes? He would guess not. She said she hadn't dated in college, but he found that impossible to believe.

She faced him. ''If you'll give me her bottle, maybe she'll drink some now.''

He handed the bottle to Mattie, aware when his fingers brushed hers, knowing he should offer to feed Elizabeth, but he wanted Mattie to stay in his room.

She swung her hips in a graceful motion that ensured the nightshirt would be tucked under her bottom as she sat down. Her knees were locked together primly. But as she settled Elizabeth, the shirt slipped up, revealing more inches of pale slender thighs.

He leaned back against a chest of drawers and crossed his legs at the ankle. Shocked by his reaction to her, he couldn't stop looking at her. She crooned softly to Elizabeth, who seemed blissfully content with her eyes closed and her tiny fingers still on the bottle. With Elizabeth cuddled against her, Mattie's nightshirt was askew so that the neckline gaped open and he saw the pale curve of a breast.

He inhaled, his body growing hot. He was stunned by his revival, startled that Mattie Ryan was the cause, worried because there was no place in his arrangement with Mattie for a mindless satisfying union of hungry flesh. But she had brought him back to life—there wasn't a shred of doubt about that. Abruptly he turned and left the room, going to the cart to get one more drink of bourbon. What had he gotten himself into with this bargain marriage? Yet the thought of Elizabeth reaffirmed that he had done the right thing. He would just have to keep his lust to himself. He tossed down a shot of bourbon, feeling it burn as he set the glass on the tray.

Filled with resolve, he inhaled, straightened his shoulders and went back to his room. Once Mattie was back in jeans and boots and her long-sleeved shirts, he would see her again as good ol' Mattie Ryan and his blood would cool.

Glancing at him as he reentered the bedroom, Mattie stood. "I'll put her in bed. She finished her bottle and she's asleep now."

He nodded and watched Mattie cross the room and lean over the bed to lay Elizabeth down. As Mattie bent over, the nightshirt hiked up inch by inch, and his temperature took a soaring leap with each inch of pale flesh exposed.

Her bottom was still covered, but his imagination was rampant. When she turned, he jerked his gaze up to meet hers, inhaling as he did so, knowing he probably should not have just thrown down a shot of bourbon. If he ever needed to keep a cool head, it was now, because nothing else about him was cool.

She crossed the room. ''Maybe it's just a new tooth.'' She picked up the bottle to hand it to him. Josh couldn't resist. His fingers closed around her wrist and he took the bottle from her hand, setting it on the chest behind him while he continued to hold her. She stared at him, her green eyes widening, a questioning look in their cool depths. Her lips parted, and he could see the pulse at her throat. He released her wrist and placed his fingers against her throat, his own pulse jumping another notch when he felt hers race.

''I'm damned thankful to have you, but I know I should be shot for binding you into a loveless marriage. Woman, you were meant for your own husband and family. You were meant for loving,'' he added in a husky voice.

Mattie's heart thudded. His hand was on her throat and his glittering eyes held a smoldering intensity that she hadn't seen before. His bass voice was raw with desire. The few times they had been together before their wedding, she wondered sometimes whether he saw her at all. Often as they sat over dinner in a restaurant, she had felt like the invisible person while he stared into space—but not now. At this moment she had his undivided attention, yet his words annoyed her and she wondered why he kept telling her what she was missing in life.

"You are absolutely the first and only man to think so," she said.

He tilted her chin higher, running his index finger along her jaw in a slow, tantalizing trail that made her tingle. Her body was responding to him in ways she had never experienced. She felt as if she was wound up tight inside, an urgency gathering in her.

"It's been a hell of a long time since I really kissed a woman."

"You kissed me today," she whispered.

He shook his head slowly, his heated gaze turning her insides to fire. "No, not really."

With a pounding heart Mattie stared at him. She couldn't imagine he had ever asked permission for a kiss in his life, yet she suspected he was on the verge of asking now. Her heart thudded against her rib cage, and her mouth became dry. All the sensible reminders popped into mind of why they should keep their arrangement business only. "I don't think—"

He leaned down, placing his mouth firmly on hers, ending her words. His tongue slipped into her mouth, and she felt as if the room had tilted and begun to whirl. Her insides heated, warmth pooling low in her and growing like a fire fanned to life. Her heart raced as she leaned closer and her tongue slipped over his.

Josh's heart thudded violently. He felt as if this tall woman—this *innocent*—was bringing him back to life with a rush like a runaway train. Her mouth was silky sleek, hot and wet and inviting. His body clenched and throbbed. His arousal was intense, and he knew he would hurt later, but right now every sensation was great. All her softness and warmth and eager responsiveness was as life-giving as oxygen for breathing. He groaned, knowing he shouldn't be kissing her. He was complicating both their lives, but he couldn't stop. Not yet. Not while her tongue was playing over his or while she was moaning softly and sliding her arms around his neck.

How good it felt to be held! He groaned again, leaning over her and kissing her deeply.

Josh's arm circled her waist, and he pulled her close. Her hands flew up against his bare chest, which was rock hard, smooth, his pectorals well-defined. He had no chest hair and her hands ran over his warm skin and solid muscles.

She moaned softly, knowing she should stop him, shocked that he wanted to kiss her after all he had said.

Instead, she stood silent, kissing him back, her fingers running lightly across his marvelous chest. Beneath her palm she could feel his heart pound, and it amazed her that she could cause such a reaction in him. He sucked her tongue deeper into his mouth as if trying to pull her into him, and while his teeth closed so gently, his tongue flicked back and forth over the tip of her tongue, inflaming her.

She had never known a man's kisses to be like Josh's, this wild storming of her senses, an awakening of forces that made her want to move closer and closer to him. Her hips shifted, thrusting against him while she moaned softly in an amazing, sweet torment.

Josh was intensely aware that all she wore was the nightshirt. He longed to slide his hands beneath it and caress her warm, silken flesh, but he could feel the reticence in her response. Common sense screamed for him to stop kissing her, yet she had been irresistible and now, even when she wasn't giving him her whole heart, her kisses were hot enough to melt him.

He longed to feel her breasts in his hands, to kiss and caress her. Already her hips were moving in a rhythm that told him as much as her kisses what effect he was having on her. And he wondered if she had the vaguest idea of what havoc she was wreaking in him. Damn, it felt so good to be free of grief, to touch and feel and be aroused!

This was a woman to stir any man's senses, to challenge him, to tempt him. Tall, shapely, full of life— Mattie made him throb with need.

Stop taking advantage of her innocence, a voice screamed at him, and he knew he should stop, but he couldn't. The woman fit perfectly in his arms. He didn't have to crouch to kiss her, and he couldn't stop thinking about her long fabulous legs.

When he felt her firm push against his chest, he released her reluctantly. Her breathing was as ragged as his. He couldn't keep from touching her and caught a long silken lock of her hair and let it slide through his fingers.

She moved out of his arms and studied him. "I thought you said you were numb, that you had no interest in sex."

"I was numb to everything when I told you that. You woke up my hormones," he said, half-amused by her frankness, more concerned with fighting the urge to reach for her again. "It's good, Mattie, to feel again," he replied with honesty. "You've brought me back to life."

She looked puzzled, as if she didn't believe him, and he wondered who had destroyed her confidence in herself as a woman.

"You had other choices," she said bluntly.

"I know I had other choices," he repeated patiently. "I did what I wanted and what I thought was best for Elizabeth. I haven't felt anything for a woman since I lost Lisa. Wanting to kiss you is a physical thing. It's nice to kiss. You're very attractive and I reacted. It's the first time in so damned long."

She frowned at him, her brow furrowing as if he had become a problem. "That's nice and thank you, but I think we need to stick to business in this arrangement."

He nodded solemnly, wondering whether she had the remotest idea how appealing she looked at the moment with her hair tumbling over her shoulders, her mouth red from his kisses. And her words were having the opposite effect on him from what she intended. With every blunt statement from her to cool his response, he wanted to reach for her and show her just what effect she could have on a man. What kind of jerk had dumped her? he wondered. Had she ever really known passion?

"Good night, Josh," she said, hurrying for her room.

He watched the switch of the shirttail across her bottom with each long step she took. "Night, Mattie. Sleep well."

She threw an exasperated look over her shoulder and left the room, closing the door behind her.

He wiped his brow and stood with his hands on his hips, staring at the closed door while his imagination ran rampant as he pictured her climbing back into bed. He shook his head. She was right, and he had better stop looking at her long legs and think about her running his household and leaving someday to go to law school.

"Hellfire," he said quietly, running his hand across the nape of his neck. He hadn't felt anything for any woman since he lost Lisa. Nothing. Now he was like a horny teenager, and Mattie hadn't done anything to cause his reaction except walk around in her unsexy nightshirt trying to be helpful.

The urges would go with daylight, he told himself, and walked to the window to stare outside, knowing he had no inclination to sleep. He ached, but it was a physical ache, a better feeling than the desolate loss that had consumed him the past months. This hurt confirmed that he was alive again. Alive and married to a woman he shouldn't touch.

Mattie lay quietly in the darkness, but her thoughts were a raging storm. Josh's kisses had shaken her and set her on fire. She had dated so little except for the few times in her freshman year in college when she had gone out with Lonny Whitaker. His kisses had never made her insides twist and her knees weak the way Josh's just had.

The man's heart is still numb and grieving even if his body isn't, she reminded herself. The attraction between them was only physical, nothing more. Josh had said so, and she knew so. Be warned, she silently admonished.

She slid out of bed and moved to the window, looking at the lights while her thoughts still seethed and her body longed for his arms. She remembered in the most vivid detail touching his chest, his mouth on hers, his tongue playing over hers, his arm tightening around her. She hadn't been married twenty-four hours and she was falling in love with him. She had always been attracted to him. Now how could she resist falling hopelessly in love with him?

She groaned and drummed her fingers on her arm nervously while she worried about the future. Think about law school, she told herself. Start making plans to take the entrance exam. She raised her chin, thinking about her busy day tomorrow and when and how she could get away to a bookstore and buy a law text.

She returned to bed, thinking about books and schedules. The next thing she knew, she opened her eyes to bright sunshine pouring into the room.

They spent the morning at the stockyards, looking at quarter horses, finally purchasing one that Mattie particularly liked. That afternoon, she remained at the hotel to interview nanny applicants while Josh returned to the stockyards.

By the time they returned to the ranch five days later, they had two new horses in tow and Mrs. Bertha Ingersoll, hired as the new nanny.

Rosalie was still working at the ranch. She had promised Josh she would stay one more week, and as soon as they arrived, she took charge of Elizabeth who laughed and held out her arms, going eagerly to Rosalie.

"Come on, Mattie, and pick out the room you want," Josh said. He draped his arm casually across her shoulders. "We'll move whatever you want from your place. I told you before and I'll say it again, your grandmother can move in here if she'd like. We have plenty of space."

"Thanks, Josh. She likes her little house and her independence. Right now, she has gone home with Carlina. When she's here, Lottie stays with her at night so she's never alone. After she gets back, I think we'll see a lot more of her because of Elizabeth."

Doors opened off both sides of the wide hallway that ran the length of the house. His arm tightened slightly as he turned her. He pointed to doors at the end of the hall. "You haven't seen this part of the house. That's Elizabeth's room and mine adjoins it. We'll look at the others."

She was aware of walking close beside him, aware of his arm across her shoulders. He touched her easily and so casually that she wondered whether he was aware of it or not. He was openly affectionate with his daughter, and Mattie guessed he was a man who liked to touch others and gave it little thought.

"If you don't have any particular choice, it might be nice to have you in the room on the other side of Elizabeth's so she's between us."

"That's fine with me."

"We'll look first."

The house was over one hundred years old, and the gleaming hardwood floors creaked as they walked from bedroom to bedroom. But the house was somewhat similar to the one she had grown up in and she felt comfortable, willing to relocate. The rooms were high ceilinged and large; the furniture was mahogany with braided rugs on the floors.

Josh showed her each room. When they reached the large bedroom that was next to Elizabeth's, Mattie stood in the center of the room and looked around. The spacious bedroom held a brass bed, marble-topped tables, a rocking chair, bookshelves and Navajo rugs on the floor. ''This room is fine for me.''

''All right. Let me show you Elizabeth's and mine.'' He tugged her arm to steer her. They looked at Elizabeth's frilly pink and white room with stuffed animals, a rocker and her baby bed. Mattie looked around, nodding approval. Josh kept his arm across her shoulders as he propelled her through the open door to his adjoining room.

She stood looking at his king-size fruitwood bed, bookshelves and desk. One wall had floor-to-ceiling mirrors, another, glass patio doors that opened onto a deck. Everywhere were pictures of his first wife, and Mattie crossed the room to pick up one from a desk. A beautiful dark-haired woman stood beside a smiling Josh. She was petite and lovely and Mattie felt a stab of sympathy for him.

''I'm sorry you lost her,'' she said quietly, replacing the picture.

He nodded, coming to stand beside her. ''I miss her,'' he said gruffly. ''But the pain is a little duller now.''

He waved his hand. ''Now you've seen the whole house,'' he said, his voice becoming brusque again. ''Tomorrow I'll show you over the ranch, and we can make some decisions about combining your place and mine. I don't want you to have to drive home every day. I think we should take down the fences between our lands.''

''Sounds reasonable to me,'' she said, still looking around his room while Josh looked at her. She was cool, collected, as businesslike as his ranch foreman, and it was disturbing him. He remembered the kiss in the hotel on their wedding night in Fort Worth. The more remote Mattie was to him, the more he wanted to break through that cool barrier she kept around herself. And at all hours during the day and night, he was finding himself speculating on what she would be like if she let down her reserve.

He wondered what was the matter with him. She was all he had dreamed and hoped for—businesslike, intelligent, coolly distant, a damned good rancher. Why couldn't he get her out of his mind? And why did he have an intense physical awareness of her? She did nothing to provoke it. Abruptly he realized she was talking to him and he hadn't heard a word she had said.

Annoyed with himself, he moved away from her. ''My mind wandered, Mattie. What did you say?''

''With the new nanny in Rosalie's house, you, Elizabeth and I will be the only ones here at night.''

''If Elizabeth doesn't sleep, I'll take care of her.''

She nodded. ''I want to see about unloading the horses. If you'll excuse me.''

''I'll go with you.''

They developed a routine, and as soon as Bertha moved into Rosalie's house and took charge of Elizabeth, Mattie began to ride with Josh during the day. And as they worked together, he realized how good she was with cows and horses.

"Damn, that woman can handle a horse as good as anyone I've ever seen!" Dusty Peterson said. Josh's foreman watched Mattie flush a recalcitrant calf out of the brush. At every turn she blocked the calf, her horse turning in an instant to work the bawling calf back toward the herd.

"She's been doing it all her life," Josh said perfunctorily, watching Mattie's trim backside in the saddle, her jeans molded to her like a second skin. He was beginning to lose sleep over the woman, and his nerves felt raw. He was finding excuses to ride with her during the day and sitting up late hours with her every night, and he knew he should stop. Yet he was drawn to her. She was all he had hoped for, plus so much more. She kept the household running smoothly, taking charge of the new cook, Maria, as well as Bertha, spending time every evening with Elizabeth and then riding like one of the men all day.

One morning in early May, while they were separating the cows from the calves, Mattie caught up with Josh to ride beside him. "I told my foreman, Abe, that I would come home at noon today and meet with him. Since I have to leave, I'll just ride with you during the morning," she said.

"Go on now if you want."

"No. I can help for a few hours."

He glanced at her. Her face looked scrubbed, her eyes bright and clear. A broad-brimmed Stetson shaded her eyes and the long braid hung down her back. "You're doing a good job, Mattie. You've got this ranch humming in order."

"Thank you. I like riding with you. I missed riding with Dad. The men who work for me are always so polite when I'm with them."

"And I'm not polite?"

She blinked, and he laughed, reaching out to tug on her braid. "I'm teasing you. Don't look so worried."

"I told you, I don't know how to deal with men on a social level."

"Why don't you?" he asked in a challenging voice. "Who's hurt you? There must have been someone." She bit her lip and gazed beyond him as she shook her head. "No one in particular. Like I told you, I've just never dated much. I've always been taller than most guys. When I was growing up, it was particularly bad. Some boys made fun of me until I didn't want to be around any of them. By the time I was a sophomore in college, I think Dad decided I would never date or marry and he began to plan my life around staying on the ranch and running it with him."

"He was too hasty."

"In college I didn't want to sleep around. That decision just added to the dating problems until I stopped going out," she said.

"So I'll bet you turned some guys down who might have been really interested."

"I might have, but it wasn't worth what I'd gone through. I've been called lots of names—in high school, 'freak' and 'geek,' and in college, just 'frigid.'"

"Hellfire," he said, staring at her as she rode with her back straight and her chin raised defiantly. He suspected her doting father hadn't helped the situation. "I'd say you survived remarkably well then."

She gave him a fleeting smile. "It wasn't a big deal after sixth or seventh grade. I spent some miserable hours in my early teens."

"Well, I'm the lucky man, thanks to the blindness of some local jerks. You would have been married long ago otherwise."

She slanted him a look, her green eyes mischievous. "Josh, you know you see me as a business partner. Before the wedding you barely knew I existed, and you probably thought of me in the same way you would one of these cowboys." Before he could answer, she urged her horse ahead, and he stared at her, his gaze dropping to her tight-fitting jeans.

There was a feisty streak in the woman that she kept under wraps most of the time, but occasionally he provoked her and it popped out. And every time she flung some challenge at him, he wanted to reach for her and taste some of that fire that seemed to simmer beneath the surface. She would be surprised to know how wrong she was, too. He did not think of her in the same way as he did any cowboy he knew. If she had any idea how much of his thoughts she was taking, she would be shocked.

As they began to round up a herd and move them to another pasture, a cow and calf cut off into the brush. Mattie went after them, turning swiftly to block the cow. As her horse spun around, a branch ripped across Mattie's cheek. The crimson slash ran from her cheek to her jaw. Josh inhaled and started to urge his horse forward when Dusty blocked his way.

"She's a damned fine cowhand. You wouldn't

come to my rescue for a scratch on the face. Don't embarrass her. She won't want special treatment.

"She's my *wife*. That's reason enough for special treatment."

Josh reined in and drew a deep breath, watching as Mattie worked the cow and calf back into the herd. Riding beside her, he pulled out a clean handkerchief and handed it to her. She stared at him blankly.

"You've cut your face."

She put her hand up and then took his handkerchief. "Thanks. I never felt it."

He stared at her, feeling a mixture of emotions. She was better than some of the men who worked for him, yet he hated the slash across her face. Her skin was soft and smooth, and she didn't belong out in the brush with cattle and horses and rough men.

Knowing that was what she preferred, he clamped his jaw closed and turned his horse.

They drove the herd to a pasture near a large wooden corral, moving quietly to cut out calves. Josh watched Mattie closely. She was competent and graceful. He admired her fine cutting horse and watched them work together as efficiently as if the horse had been an extension of her.

An hour later he glanced back to see Mattie wheel her horse around and head back toward the house. He watched her, thinking of moments with her, admitting to himself he'd been looking forward all day to their evening together.

Six

Mattie brushed down, fed and watered her bay before striding to the house. Noonday sun was blistering and a dust devil swirled in the pasture to her right. As she neared the back door she heard screams.

Frowning, Mattie quickened her step and entered the cool house. Elizabeth's shrieks were louder and above the commotion Bertha Ingersoll shouted.

"Shut up! Just shut up your crying!"

Horrified, Mattie raced to the family room and charged through the door. Elizabeth sat sobbing in the middle of the floor while Bertha was sprawled in a leather chair, her feet on an ottoman. She was shaking her finger at Elizabeth.

"Elizabeth," Mattie said, rushing in to sweep the child into her arms.

"Mrs. Brand!" Bertha came to her feet as Mattie whirled around.

"I thought we fully understood each other about punishing Elizabeth or screaming at her."

"Ma'am, she's just cranky."

"So am I," Mattie snapped while she held a shaking Elizabeth who clung to her. The baby was hot and damp from crying. "Did you hit her?"

"Heavens, no! Although she could use a good swat."

"No, she could not."

"I'll take her. It was just temperament—"

"Your job is terminated," Mattie said quietly.

"That's ridiculous! Child is spoiled rotten—"

"I don't know how you got such excellent references, but I'll not have you yelling at Elizabeth. And this sweet child isn't spoiled. You'll be paid for two weeks, but you need to pack and leave. You're through now."

"You can't fire me over a child crying! There's—"

"Goodbye, Bertha," Mattie said, her voice growing quiet.

Bertha opened her mouth, looked into Mattie's eyes and turned on her heel, leaving the room.

"Shh, I'm here, love," Mattie whispered, jiggling Elizabeth. Mattie patted the baby's back, turned off the television and went to the nursery to rock her.

In minutes Elizabeth was quiet, and Mattie went to the phone to call her ranch and talk to her foreman.

After the phone call she bathed and changed Elizabeth, fed her lunch and then buckled her into the car seat. She was taking Elizabeth with her to the Rocking R. Two hours later she drove home with Elizabeth, talking to her as they sped to the Triple B.

Elizabeth went down for a nap easily, and Mattie

picked up the toys in the family room. When Maria came into the kitchen to start dinner, Mattie offered to help.

Maria was married to one of the hands, she and her husband, Charley Adair, had a small house on the ranch. Maria cooked and cleaned now, coming in late afternoon during the week. She did not work on weekends.

Mattie helped Maria for a few minutes and then went up to wash and change for dinner. She dressed in cutoffs and a blue shirt before brushing and braiding her hair again. While she moved around the room restlessly, waiting for Josh's arrival, Gran called. As Mattie talked on the phone, Josh passed her room, but it was another ten minutes before she hung up the phone and went to his room. The door stood open, and she went inside.

"Josh?"

He stepped out of his bathroom, a towel fastened around his waist. Startled, Mattie's gaze ran down the length of him. His skin was dark, his body tightly muscled, and the white towel was a stark contrast wrapped low around his slender hips.

"Sorry to intrude."

"Come in. I've got on a towel," he said, and she heard the amusement in his voice. Mattie drew a deep breath at the sight of him. His dark eyes flicked over her, and he crossed the room, reaching around her to close the door. He stopped only a few feet from her, his hands on his hips. "You look cool and nice."

"Thank you," she said, momentarily distracted. She realized he was beginning to notice her more, just as she noticed him now. His black hair was damp, sleeked back from his face. He was almost nude, incredibly masculine and handsome. Her pulse raced, and she struggled to stop staring at his body.

"How's the cut?" he asked, touching her jaw with the tip of his finger and turning her face to look at her cheek.

"It'll mend in a few days," she replied. She was too conscious of his magnificent body, of him stroking her cheek.

"And how are things at your place?" he said, standing too close, looking at her too intently.

Mattie couldn't keep her gaze from drifting down over his chest again, remembering that moment in the hotel in Fort Worth when he had pulled her into his arms and kissed her.

"Mattie?"

She realized he said her name and she looked up. While his dark gaze searched hers, tension arced between them like lightning. The air all but crackled while her nerves became raw.

Josh stared at her, feeling as if he could get lost in the green depths of her eyes. She was in cutoffs and a fresh shirt, with only the slightest makeup on her face. She looked gorgeous, but it was the expression in her eyes that had him going up in flames. For four weeks now they had lived under the same roof, getting up at night with Elizabeth, riding together, bumping into each other in moments like this one. He had seen Mattie in her cotton nightgown, seen her asleep in a T-shirt, brushed against her too many times a day to count, and it was all building an awareness in him that was tying him in knots. His gaze lowered to her full lips which parted, and he remembered their softness, the sweet, hot wetness of her mouth.

Now her wide green eyes were an irresistible invitation. With a groan, he slipped an arm around her narrow waist and pulled her against him. She smelled like roses and was so soft it made him tremble. There was no mistaking the hunger and want in her eyes.

Bending his head, he covered her mouth with his. His tongue met hers, slipped deep into her mouth, tasting her fiery sweetness while he tightened his hold and pulled her closer. He wanted this woman with a need that startled and shook him. Her hands rested against his shoulders and then slipped around his neck and he groaned, relishing the marvel of her holding him. How good her soft body, her soft touch felt!

Mattie clung to him, her heart pounding while she followed his lead, returning his kiss, her tongue sliding into his mouth. His arms tightened until she wondered whether she could get another breath, yet she loved being held by him, feeling his solid muscles, his lean strength. Slowly, conscious of the line she was crossing and the barrier she was lowering between them, she slid her fingers down his smooth, strong back. She felt his narrow waist, the rough texture of the towel that was knotted tightly around him. And she felt his hard masculinity press against her, bold evidence of the effect she was having on him.

Heat coiled low in her body, a driving need that was agony. She wanted to thrust her hips against him. She was bombarded by sensations new to her, sensations that were as intoxicating as the strongest wine.

Wanting her, Josh leaned away slightly, tugging her shirt out of her shorts and running his hand beneath it. When he cupped her breast, Mattie felt as if she would melt with pleasure. He pushed aside the lace, his thumb flicking over her nipple while he kissed her hard.

She moaned, the sound taken by his mouth. He released her, and she gasped for breath, momentarily startled that his arms were gone from around her. Then she felt his fingers at her buttons. His dark eyes made her tremble, because his desire was blatant and scalding. As he pushed away her shirt, she felt the heat flood her cheeks, yet she couldn't stop him. Instead, her breasts tingled and her body ached with a longing that she had never felt before.

"You're beautiful," he said in a raspy voice while he cupped her breasts in his dark hands, his thumbs circling her nipples. Pleasure swept over her, and she ached for more. The hungry desire in the midnight depths of Josh's eyes shook her.

She should stop him. She knew this held little meaning for him beyond something physical, yet she couldn't stop him. His caresses were monumental to her. He was sexy, damned handsome, so confident. He could have had most any woman he wanted, yet to have him tell her she was beautiful and look at her as if she were the only woman in the world, was intoxicating, too irresistible to tell him to stop.

She looked at him through half-closed eyes, relishing his body, glorying that he wanted her. He leaned down, taking her nipple in his mouth, stroking her with his tongue. With a small cry, she reached for him, sliding her arms around his neck again and moving close to kiss him.

His arms wrapped around her like tight bands. She

kissed him, letting go the pent-up yearning, memorizing the moment. Her body fit perfectly against the hard contours of his body; the bulge of his manhood pressed against her, and she thrilled to the feel of him against her body.

Knowing it was all moving too fast for her, she found the courage to resist, pushing away. She stepped back, pulling her blouse closed. "We weren't going to do this," she whispered. "Our lives will part, Josh. I don't know how to be casual about sex." Trying to get strength into her voice, she struggled at the same time to keep her gaze from sliding over him.

She wanted him to say that they wouldn't part, to deny that he would let her go sometime in the future, yet he stood watching her in silence. She averted her eyes. But in her peripheral vision, she could see the white towel and the effects of their kisses. He was as aroused as she was, yet any loving would be meaningless to him, she knew.

Disappointed, still wanting him, she turned her back and fastened her bra and began buttoning her wrinkled shirt, while her thoughts roiled like a storm-swept sea.

As badly as she desired him, she couldn't go into a meaningless, physical relationship. When he finally said it was over, it would tear her apart. And there was no doubt that someday a physical relationship with Josh would be completely over.

Her fingers shook as she buttoned her blouse. He was so quiet, she wondered what he was thinking.

"You're a very desirable, beautiful woman, Mattie," he said, his voice a husky rasp. She closed her eyes, feeling torn, wanting to turn around and fling herself in his arms and try to make him fall in love with her. But that was exactly what the nannies before her had done and they'd completely turned him off. He wouldn't fall in love with her that way. They lived under the same roof, rode together all day, talked with each other every evening. They were both normal, healthy and strong. The proximity was bound to ignite fires between them, but it didn't mean it would create love.

"Thank you," Mattie said firmly, wishing her thudding heart would slow and her nerves would calm and her memory would forget his kisses and caresses.

He moved past her, picked up his jeans and disappeared into the bathroom. Minutes later, he reappeared, wearing his jeans, buttoning the last button. He sucked in his narrow waist and she watched, fascinated by him.

She felt on fire with the longing to feel his strong, hard body pressed against her again. His skin was the color of teak, and his muscles rippled as he walked. She looked up and found him watching her.

"I came in to talk to you," she said, trying to get her mind back on the problems at hand, to stop being so conscious of his bare chest.

"And?" he asked after a moment.

Momentarily she forgot completely what she was about to say. She tried to recall why she was in his room. He was waiting, watching her closely. "You distract me!" she said, impatient with herself.

"I'm glad," he answered quietly. "It's good to know you notice me."

"I've always noticed you. And I have to talk to you," she added swiftly as his brows arched and he opened his mouth to say something. "When I came home today, Bertha was yelling at Elizabeth. I fired the woman.''

''Hellfire.'' Frowning, he rubbed the back of his neck. ''I don't want to say I told you so, but I've had nothing except trouble with nannies. She didn't hurt Elizabeth, did she?''

''No, I don't think so. Elizabeth has never acted as if she didn't like her or was scared of her. Bertha was yelling, but she was in the chair watching television. She said she had never struck Elizabeth, and I think she was telling the truth. I can't understand her excellent references. How could she have had such good references?''

''If all she does is yell, maybe the family we talked to didn't mind her shouting at their kids. She worked for them eight years, so they should have known her.''

''Eight years is a long time, and they thought she was wonderful. Anyway, I'll get someone else.''

''I can ask Maria to keep Elizabeth during the day until we find another nanny.''

Mattie shook her head. ''No need. I'll stay with Elizabeth until you hire someone.''

His brows arched. ''You're sure?''

''I think I can give up riding after bawling cows and calves for a few days,'' she said, touching the cut on her cheek lightly.

He moved closer and with every step she felt her pulse jump another notch. ''Josh—'' she said, her tone of voice holding a warning that stopped him.

''You're certain Elizabeth is all right?''

''Yes, she's fine. She was playing almost as soon as we got home.'' Mattie moved away, hurrying toward the door. "I'll see you at dinner. I'll help Maria so she can go home early."

The door closed behind her, and he stood with his fists on his hips. He wanted Mattie, and his desire was escalating fiercely. He closed his eyes, remembering the past few moments. "Hellfire," he swore softly, striding impatiently to the closet to get his shirt. He knew Mattie had ordered texts to study for the entrance exam to law school. She was already thinking about the day she would pack and go.

He thought about really courting her, trying to win her affections, to get her to stay, but the moment the idea came to mind, he rejected it. He wouldn't make the same mistakes a second time. He had argued and cajoled and coaxed Lisa into staying on the ranch. If he hadn't, she would be alive today.

When the time came, he had to let Mattie go. Right now, he was damn lucky to have her, and he should keep his hands to himself, he admonished. He tried to remember her in years past, but he had barely noticed her then. And whenever he thought of her in earlier years, he always pictured her at her father's side. Even in barrel racing, her dad was always waiting in the wings, always watching her.

Josh thought about Elizabeth. Was he going to be a father like Frank Ryan? Someday he would have to let Elizabeth go, too. He hoped he didn't turn possessive like Old Man Ryan.

Josh yanked on his shirt and combed his hair. In the mirror's reflection he noticed the faint smudges of red on his mouth and he carefully wiped them away. Mattie was some woman, and he was going to have to exercise more good sense and control around her.

She was his *wife,* dammit, and as off-limits to him as if she were married to someone else. She was a wife in name only, and he was the only one to blame. But if he had known, would he have waited and courted her and really tried to win her over?

While he mulled the question, he stared at himself in the mirror. He shook his head. He wasn't in love with her. He still loved Lisa, but he wanted Mattie. His body ached for her. It was lust, but there was more to it than that. A lot more. He liked her. She was turning into one of the best friends he'd had. She was easier to talk to than Lisa had been, but then Mattie knew his world. He couldn't imagine any problem he couldn't discuss with her.

"Except that I want to go to bed with you," he said aloud, thinking about her big green eyes staring at him.

"Hellfire. The woman's got me talking to myself, forgetting tasks, shaking like I'm one hundred years old." He turned abruptly and strode down the hall toward the kitchen.

Mattie looked up when he entered. Her green eyes sparkled and she held a manual in her hand. Brown wrapping paper was strewn on the countertop.

"Look, my law texts came! Here are the manuals I sent for so I can study for the LSAT, the Law School Admission Test."

"Now you'll be studying at night."

"I can study when you work on your bookkeeping." She stacked the manuals on the counter. "I told Gran I wanted to go to law school."

"What did she say?" he asked, looking at the eagerness in Mattie's expression, wanting to cross the room and toss the books aside and pull her into his arms and make love to her.

"She asked what *you* thought. I think anything that's all right with you is fine with her. She is so happy I'm married. Gran never did want me to work alongside Dad."

Only half listening to her, Josh couldn't resist the temptation to cross the room, placing his hand on the counter and leaning close to her. "Then she might not be hurt if you gave up the ranch."

"She would be hurt if I sold it. As long as it stays in the family and I'm your wife, she's happy."

"So am I, Mattie."

Mattie inhaled deeply. "Josh, you stand too close. Dinner's ready as soon as Elizabeth wakes."

"You make me want to stand close—"

A wail came from down the hall and Mattie brushed past him. "I'll go get Elizabeth."

He watched the sway of her hips and swore at himself. Leave the woman alone, he told himself again, turning to glare at the law manuals.

That night after dinner they took Elizabeth outside. Josh put up a baby swing on a low branch of a tall oak while Elizabeth played in the grass and Mattie alternately watched her and her daddy.

Muscles flexed in his arms and back as he worked on the swing. He hoisted himself up into the tree, climbing out onto a branch to fasten chains over it. He slipped the protective rubber coverings in place on the chains to protect the tree limb and then he dropped easily to the ground.

"Ma," Elizabeth said, holding up her arms.

Startled because Elizabeth had never called her any

name, Mattie knelt down to pick her up. "It's Mattie, Elizabeth. Ma-tee," she enunciated.

"You may have to settle for Ma," Josh said quietly.

"I'm not her mother, and I don't want her to call me something that will upset you."

"It won't upset me. I imagine before long she'll be calling you Mama. She's too little to remember Lisa," he said in a pained voice. "When she's old enough, I'll tell her about her mother. I tell her off and on now, but it's meaningless."

"It might not be so meaningless. She's a very bright child."

"You think so?" he asked, studying Mattie intently.

"Yes, very," she said, looking at Elizabeth who was untying the ribbon around Mattie's braid. "You are a bright girl, aren't you, Li'l Bit?"

"Are you coming?" Mattie asked, slanting Josh a look over her shoulder as she and Elizabeth headed toward the barn.

"Sure. I'll finish the swing in a little while." He watched her head toward the gate while he felt a surge of satisfaction. Mattie and Elizabeth had taken to each other like a lost kitten and its mother. Mattie fussed over her, played with her and paid more attention to her every day. Elizabeth, in turn, was reaching for Mattie more and more often. He wondered whether Mattie noticed their changing relationship or not.

As he strode across the yard to catch up with them, he watched the sway of Mattie's hips again and swore at himself. *Leave the woman alone,* he warned himself. *She's only in your life temporarily.*

Josh tried. For the last two weeks of May, he really tried to avoid spending time with Mattie. They stopped riding together because now she stayed home with Elizabeth. He missed her company, reminding himself that her absence would only be for about a week or two while she ran ads and interviewed nannies and hired someone. When he was with her, he tried to keep his hands to himself. He tried to avoid spending every spare moment with her, but by the end of two weeks, he was back to looking forward eagerly to the early evening hours when they both played with Elizabeth and then the quiet hours of companionship with Mattie after Elizabeth was tucked into bed.

And avoiding her had not diminished his need to be with her one degree. To his chagrin, he thought about her more than ever.

On a hot afternoon the last week of June, while riding beside Dusty as they headed home, he was lost in thought until he noticed Dusty staring at him, his blue eyes filled with curiosity.

"Something wrong?" Josh asked. "Have I just turned green or something?"

"Maybe I ought to ask *you,* boss. I've known you a long time. Is something wrong?"

"No. Everything's fine. What made you ask?"

"I've asked you a coupla questions and haven't gotten any answers."

Josh gritted his teeth. "Sorry. My mind was on Elizabeth. I've been up nights with her. I think she's getting a new tooth." He was flat lying to Dusty, but how could he explain he was awake hours during the night because he wanted his wife?

"How's the missus?"

"Mattie's fine."

"Miss her out here riding with us. You're a fortunate man. You deserve a fine woman, but you're real lucky."

"I know I'm lucky." They reached the corral and dismounted, each taking care of his horse in silence. When Josh was ready to head for the house, he glanced over his shoulder. "See you, Dusty."

"Sure. Hope you sleep tonight. And hope Li'l Bit gets her tooth."

"Thanks."

Josh crossed the yard, puffs of dust rising after each step. He raised his hat and wiped sweat off his forehead. It had to be over one hundred degrees. All he wanted was a cold shower, a cold beer and a long quiet evening with Mattie. He closed his thoughts beyond that, fighting images that taunted and threatened his fragile peace. He could remember that day in his bedroom when he had unbuttoned her shirt. She was beautiful with full, lush curves, so soft it made him quiver to think about her.

Inside the cool house it was quiet. Maria was nowhere in sight, yet the kitchen smelled tantalizing. He tossed his hat on a peg and went to the fridge. A bowl of fresh fruit and a platter of chicken salad looked tempting. He grabbed a beer, uncapped it and yanked out his shirttail as he headed down the hall.

"Mattie! Li'l Bit! I'm home!"

He took a long drink, feeling the cold beer go down. He pulled the bandana from around his neck, wiped his forehead again and yanked off his shirt. He looked into the empty family room. Where was everyone?

He headed toward his room. "Mattie!"

No answer. His curiosity rose until he heard a

squeal of laughter. Following the sounds, he headed toward Mattie's room. Loud splashing and shrieks came from Elizabeth. And Mattie's laughter rang out, a sound that lifted his spirits.

He leaned against the jamb of Mattie's bathroom doorway, enjoying the sight of Mattie bathing Elizabeth. Elizabeth's hair was sudsy, standing straight up in a point. Mattie was in cutoffs, her shirt tied high around her midriff and unbuttoned low in front, and she was barefoot. She had looped her hair on her head, but short tendrils escaped around her face, hanging over her ears and neck. The front of her shirt was soaked, suds were on her cheek, and she was laughing as she bathed Elizabeth who was splashing water wildly with both hands.

Leaning over the edge of the tub, Mattie rose to her knees, her bottom trim in the tight cutoffs. Josh drew a deep breath as he stared at her.

Mattie rubbed Elizabeth's head. "Now, I'm ready to rinse your hair. It will be so easy, Li'l Bit. Here's your yellow duck that goes *quack quack,*" Mattie said, trying to distract Elizabeth while she rinsed the soap out of her hair.

She almost had it rinsed when Elizabeth realized what she was doing. "No!" she screeched, trying to pull away.

"Look at him," Mattie said, swishing the yellow plastic duck through the water. "He's looking for his mama. *Quack, quack!*"

Elizabeth laughed, forgetting about the rinsing. She splashed the duck, suddenly splashing Mattie. "Mama!"

"Hey, you," Mattie said good-naturedly, a thrill

thumping in her heart when Elizabeth called her Mama.

Elizabeth smiled up at her. "Mama."

"Yes, Li'l Bit? You're a sweetie, did you know that? You're my little sweetie, and you're also your daddy's little sweetie. We'll get you out now," she said, lifting Elizabeth from the tub, then drying her off before placing her in the bassinet.

"Knock, knock. Can I come in!" Josh rapped on the jamb.

"Josh! I didn't know it was so late—"

Mattie looked flustered, and Josh wondered if she thought she didn't look presentable, because she reached up to push locks of hair away from her face. Bending forward, he turned on a bathtub faucet and tugged off a dusty boot.

"If that is cold water," he began, tossing down the boot and pulling off the other one with a grunt of effort. He flung it aside and yanked off his socks. "I'm getting in it," he stated, throwing down his shirt, setting the beer on the vanity and stepping into the tub.

"Josh!" Mattie exclaimed. "Your jeans!"

"I almost threw myself into the horse trough, it was so damned hot outside," he said as he sank into the water then submerged himself, coming up at once and shaking his hair away from his face.

"Well, you can have the tub. You don't need me," Mattie said. She sounded breathless, and he looked at her to find her studying his chest.

Cool water swirled around him. He grabbed Mattie's wrist, feeling devilish, curious about the change in her tone, throwing his resolutions to leave her alone to the winds. "Come in with me," he said.

Mattie looked at the gleam in Josh's eyes and struggled to break free. "Don't be ridiculous."

"Come on, Mattie," he urged. "For once in your life, turn loose and do something silly."

"I'm not getting in the tub like this!" she protested, laughing, but still struggling with him, seeing laughter dancing in his dark eyes.

With a splash of water that went over the floor and Mattie, Josh stood, stepped out of the tub and scooped Mattie into his arms.

"Josh Brand, put me down!"

"Sure will," he drawled and sat down in the tub. He reached around her to turn off the faucet. "Now we can cool off together," he said.

"Josh Brand, look at me! You've lost your mind!" Mattie exclaimed.

"You look better than that dinner I saw in the fridge," he remarked, and Mattie turned her head to meet his gaze. She was in his arms in the tub. His chest was bare and her left hand was against him, her right arm still around his neck from when he had lifted her into his arms. She met his dark eyes, and her breathing stopped as she stared at him.

The laughter vanished in his eyes, replaced instantly by desire. He ran his finger along the edge of her shirt, down over her curves. Her heart pounded, and she drew a deep breath, feeling tingles from his touch, aware of their wet bodies pressed together, of his arousal against her thigh, of his hand resting on her hip.

She caught his hand. "Josh, I don't think this is a good idea."

"I suppose you're right," he admitted reluctantly.

She stood, and water poured off her. "When I get out of the tub, I'll get water all over everything. And you will, too."

"Okay. I shouldn't have done this, but it feels like heaven. It's hotter than Hades out there today. There's no need to trail water into the bedroom. Go ahead and strip down here in the bathroom. I'll turn my head."

Annoyed, Mattie stared at him. Elizabeth was happily playing in her bassinet. Josh leaned back, his arms spread over the back of the tub. His head was wet, his hair sleeked back, drops of water glistening on his shoulders and chest. He looked too damned appealing and sexy. She inhaled and grabbed a towel. "All right. Turn your head."

"Reluctantly," he said and turned his face to the wall.

"Close your eyes."

His lashes lowered and her gaze ran over him swiftly, her pulse jumping at the sight of his broad chest, glistening with water. Why did the man have to have a body that made her weak in the knees? And he was beginning to lose his somber preoccupation with grief. A forceful, dynamic personality was surfacing that made him doubly irresistible. He had filled voids in her empty life, and she was more drawn to him with every day, yet caution warned her to be careful.

She stepped out of the tub. Holding the towel, she turned around to strip down to her underwear.

Josh opened his eyes. He had made all sorts of vows and promises to Mattie, but turning his head and closing his eyes were not hard-and-fast guarantees.

Unabashed, he looked at her, and his cool body

blazed into another sweat that was hotter than the one caused outside by the blazing sun. Mattie had her back to him and was stepping out of her cutoffs. Her filmy pink panties clung wetly to her shapely bottom, which was more enticing and sexy than he had imagined. She dropped the blouse, and his gaze ran down her slender back that narrowed to a tiny waist, then flared out slightly at her hips and round bottom. He looked at her long shapely legs, sleek and wet from the bath, and his arousal was hard and hot.

He turned his head before she caught him looking, but he knew he would have the image of her indelibly etched in his mind forever. The woman was to-die-for gorgeous. Lush, smooth, sexy. He wanted her more than ever.

When the bathroom door closed, he looked around again. She was gone and had taken Elizabeth with her. He ran his hand over his head, then slipped beneath the water and came up swiftly, splashing more bathwater on the floor.

He stepped out, grabbed a clean towel and yanked off his jeans and shorts, knotting the towel around his waist. He knocked on the closed bathroom door, adjoining Mattie's bedroom. "Mattie, can I come out of here?"

"Sure."

He opened the door. Elizabeth sat in her carrier. Mattie was dressed in a cotton sundress and was starting to braid her hair. He couldn't resist looking at her from her head to her toes. The dress was blue denim with a square neckline and narrow straps over her bare shoulders. It had patch pockets on the skirt. "You look great!" he exclaimed in a husky voice.

She blushed as she faced him, then ran her hand over her skirt nervously. "I don't have many dresses. I bought this last weekend when we were in town and I was shopping for Elizabeth."

"I like it. It could be shorter."

Frowning, she looked down. "It's too long?"

"I can't see enough of your legs."

Her head came up, and he bit back a smile at the surprise in her wide eyes. "You had me worried. I'm not very sure of myself when it comes to dresses—something my sisters mastered at age five."

"You're doing fine. Just remember shorter next time," he added lightly, and she made a face at him.

With a kiss for Elizabeth, he left to shower and change, his thoughts of Mattie seething while the image of her stepping out of the wet cutoffs stayed firmly in his mind.

As he was dressing after his shower, his gaze paused on Lisa's picture. He crossed the room to pick up the photo, looking at her smiling face. "I love you," he said softly. "I've got a good woman, Lisa. I have to go on with life. She's so good to Li'l Bit." He replaced the picture. The loss still hurt. He would love Lisa always and love the memories he had, but the pain had dulled and his grief was healing and he knew why it was healing. Mattie. A woman who would be part of his life even more briefly than Lisa had been.

He glanced around the room that was filled with pictures of Lisa. Even if it was temporary, he was married to another woman now. He picked up the pictures carefully and carried them to the closet, slowly putting most of them away. There was one in Elizabeth's room, and he would leave it there. Elizabeth should grow up knowing what her mother looked like. But Mattie shouldn't have to face his first wife's picture everywhere she turned.

Josh joined Mattie and Elizabeth in the dining room, and they shared a quiet dinner. He told Mattie about his day—which fences were down, that a faulty water pump needed to be fixed—then he leaned back in his chair and sipped his iced tea. "Have you had any responses to the ad for a nanny?"

Mattie was feeding the baby mashed carrots, carefully wiping her chin, while Elizabeth was busily trying to pick up bits of a banana that Mattie had cut up for her. Mattie glanced at him, her look direct and unwavering. "I didn't place the ad."

Seven

"Why didn't you run the ad?"

"I rather like the way we're living right now," she answered quietly, concentrating on spooning another bit of carrot into Elizabeth's mouth.

Startled, he stared at her, remembering those first few times together when she had sworn she couldn't take care of Elizabeth. Yet she had stepped in and taken charge of Elizabeth with quiet efficiency. And he knew Elizabeth was coming to love Mattie. He felt a pang. How much would it hurt Elizabeth when Mattie left them?

"I thought you didn't want to take care of a child," he said quietly.

She sent him a look that he couldn't fathom before she turned her attention back to Elizabeth. "You have an adorable daughter," she said, more to Elizabeth than to him. "I enjoy this, so I'll just stay with her."

"What about studying for law school?" he asked, holding his breath.

"Oh, I've been studying for the exam. I can read while she's napping and at night. And I've applied to take the LSAT in Austin." She paused to look at him. "I can get Lottie to watch Elizabeth the day I'm gone. It's scheduled for next Monday."

"That's right away," he said. "Planning on getting out of our marriage?"

"Of course not. I just thought I'd get the preliminaries out of the way. I might not pass the test."

"You'll pass the test. I saw your college transcript. You had an *A* average." Feeling a strange knot inside, he knew it was going to hurt when she did go. He leaned back in his chair and watched her feed Elizabeth while images of her shedding her cutoffs plagued him.

She glanced at him. "So what are you thinking?"

"If you stay regularly with Elizabeth, what happens when you leave? Elizabeth may come to love you very much."

"I thought about that, but even if I get a nanny she likes, there's no guarantee the nanny will stay. Elizabeth will have to make adjustments like that all through life. Of course, if you don't want me to stay with her—"

"Damn straight! I want you to stay!" he said emphatically, leaning forward. "You're the best one to have with her. Every day we have you, we'll be lucky," he said, his voice becoming husky, thinking about himself.

She glanced at him again, curiosity in her gaze, and he stared back. He wanted her. Half the time—more than half—he wanted to pull her into his arms. He struggled with himself now to keep from going around the table and taking her into his arms; he had sworn he would try to keep his hands to himself. Mattie had single-handedly vanquished his grief and loneliness. He noticed the world around him again, felt as if he were emerging out of dark depths into sunshine. Elizabeth and Mattie brought warmth to him, but it was Mattie who was giving vitality to his life.

"Then that's settled," she said, returning to feeding Elizabeth.

After dinner, Josh took his daughter outside to carry her around the yard and down to the barn. Mattie cleaned the kitchen and watched his long stride, inhaling deeply. *Every day we have you, we'll be lucky.* His words played in her thoughts. If only he meant them with his whole heart, but she knew there was still a part of him locked away tightly, and she knew she wasn't going to be the woman to win his heart.

That night after they had tucked Elizabeth into bed, they sat talking in the family room. Long past midnight a rumble in the distance made both of them stop and listen.

"Thunder," Josh said, standing to go to the window. "I hope to hell it isn't just the heat." He went back to sprawl on the sofa while Mattie sat on the floor, trying to organize a baby book for Elizabeth.

"When was this picture taken?"

He rolled off the sofa and went to sit beside her on the floor, looking at Elizabeth's baby picture and inhaling Mattie's perfume. "I don't remember. Mom was always writing me for pictures—" He stopped and shook his head, then stood and crossed the room. "I forgot something I have to tell you."

Josh picked up a letter from his desk, then returned to sit beside her. "This is from Mom. She wants us to come to Chicago with Elizabeth next month, around August fifteenth."

"That's fine."

"Good. I'll let her know we'll be there. I'll warn you now—Mom will have a party every night we're there. She'll want to introduce you to all their friends."

Mattie turned to ice as she twisted around to face him. "I can't do that."

"Why not?"

She straightened. "I don't know anything about parties, Josh. That's so out of my element. I never socialized. Dad and I just stayed at the ranch. He didn't like parties, and after Mom died he turned down most invitations. I told you, in some ways I feel like an anachronism."

Josh scooted closer beside her and rested his arms on her shoulders. He caught her long braid in his hands behind her head, toying with it while he gazed into worried green eyes.

"You'll do fine. It won't be as big a deal as our wedding reception."

"Oh, yes, it will," she said firmly. He could detect the scent of roses, and he was conscious of his knee touching her thigh, his arms resting on her slender shoulders. He began to unfasten her braid. "It's nothing to you, and you can't understand why I'd be afraid," she continued, "but I don't have fancy dresses—I hardly have any dresses. Besides the one

I'm wearing now, I have two old dresses and one from the rehearsal dinner we had. That's it.''

"Don't worry. We can get you dresses.''

"You know it's more than that. I don't know how to mix and mingle with people—especially when it's senators and legislators and big-city people like the ones your mother and stepfather know.''

"I'm not worried, and you shouldn't be. Just be yourself.
They won't be any different from people here, Mattie.''

"I'll be a hick. And not only a hick, but a six-foot-tall one.''

"How in the hell did you get the idea that you're too tall?''

"I am! Dad always said I was just too tall for boys.''

"Well, did it ever occur to you that your dad might have been wrong?''

"No, he wasn't,'' she said, staring solemnly at him. Josh carefully and slowly unfastened her braid. He combed his fingers through her hair and let the locks fall over her shoulders. Through a haze of worries, Mattie was aware of his warm fingers brushing her shoulders and throat, tugging lightly at strands of her hair. She stared into his dark eyes while her thoughts churned at the prospect of having to attend several big-city parties.

"I think your dad was way off base. And I think he caused you to sell yourself short.''

"You don't know what I went through growing up. No one does.''

"But you're all grown up and a beautiful woman,''

Josh said in a husky voice. He ran his fingers along the edge of the straps of her dress, feeling her smooth warm skin while he stared at her. He was only inches from her, and he wanted to kiss her.

''Josh—''

He leaned the last inches and covered her mouth with his. The moment his tongue went deeply into her mouth, his body tightened. He slipped his arm around her waist and pulled her around to cradle her against his shoulder while he kissed away the protest he knew was coming.

Mattie closed her eyes and wrapped her arms around his neck while she returned his kisses. Why couldn't she resist him? But she knew the answer. He was sexy, handsome, experienced, and she was vulnerable and couldn't resist a man like him. She had no illusions. He was not falling in love with her. There were still too many moments when he looked incredibly sad or pained and she knew he was remembering and grieving for his first wife. Josh's desire for her was physical, a need growing out of sheer proximity. He was a healthy, strong male with normal urges.

Josh's hand slid along her leg, and then beneath the full skirt of her sundress. All her logic vanished as he stroked her bare leg, his fingers moving so lightly over her knee, along her thigh. She caught his wrist and tugged his hand away, and he wrapped his arms around her, holding her while he kissed her.

While his fingers stroked her back, a fiery heat built within her. Fighting inner battles, yet unable to resist, she wound her fingers in his thick hair, sliding her hand beneath his shirt to touch his shoulders.

He twisted free the buttons in the back of her dress

and pushed the sundress down. With a moan she arched her back while his hand cupped her breast and his thumb circled the nipple. She felt dizzy with desire, wanting him, unable to stop him, knowing every touch bound her more deeply to him.

He twisted around and lowered her to the floor, leaning down to kiss her breast. She gasped with pleasure, her hands winding in his hair. She wanted him more each time they kissed, and each time she found it more difficult to tell him to stop. He shifted between her legs, pushing up her skirt as he trailed his tongue in a fiery path along her inner thigh.

Feeling as if she had lost control of her body, she arched her hips. She knew nothing about being loved by a man and she wanted this knowledge. She wanted to know what it was like with Josh. And she wanted to touch and feel and memorize him, to know him and store away memories of their moments together. She twisted the buttons of his shirt and pushed it open to run her hands over his marvelous chest.

His hand stroked her, his fingers sliding beneath the flimsy panties, and she cried out with pleasure as she moved against the pressure that consumed her. And she knew she had let passion go way too far. How much of her heart was she giving with each kiss?

"Josh!" She scrambled away from him, pulling at her dress. Standing, she moved away while she tried to catch her breath. Her heart pounded, and her body was on fire with longing. She wanted him desperately, yet she didn't want to get hurt badly.

She glanced over her shoulder at him, and her heart thudded at the desire in his expression. "I can't go into a relationship lightly."

"You're a little late. We're married."

"But our marriage isn't real, and it's not going to last."

He stared at her while she held her breath, waiting, wanting to hear a declaration of love from him even though she knew it was ridiculous to harbor such hope.

"I want you," he said gruffly.

"That's not enough. Too much is involved. If I make a commitment, you know it'll be forever."

Fighting the urge to reach for her to try to seduce her and destroy all her arguments, Josh stared at her. She didn't want to live on a ranch any more than Lisa had. Mattie had her law manuals, and in a week she would take the LSAT, preparing herself for when she would leave him.

Hurting, he rose abruptly and went outside, then stood on the porch and watched the lightning in the distance and the mounds of clouds banked along the horizon. A gust of hot wind struck him, carrying dust and the faint smell of rain.

"Josh?"

As Mattie joined him, he placed his arm around her shoulders. "I'll respect what you want, Mattie, but sometimes, I'm going to slip."

She couldn't think of anything to answer and stood quietly watching the lightning in the distance. The warm air carried cool drafts as gusts blew across the porch. She watched the storm brew, but was far more aware of her own stormy thoughts as Josh held her close against his side. Even this slight thing—just standing beside him on the porch with his arm across her shoulders—felt so good, so right. She felt as if she had come home. If only he could let go his memories and love her. But she had learned years ago to stop dreaming of "if onlys."

"Let's go in and you can read Mom's letter," he said.

Josh dropped his arm, and they entered the house. Bracing for the coming storm that would take place only a few feet away, he handed her the letter and sprawled on the sofa while she read.

Mattie's head came up, her eyes narrowing. "We can't do this!" She waved the letter at him.

"Do what?" he asked, although he knew perfectly well what she referred to.

"'We've done over the guest rooms,'" Mattie read aloud, "'and the big one is for you and Mattie. The smaller one now has a baby bed ready for Elizabeth.'" Mattie lowered the letter. "You and I can't share a bedroom."

He held out his hands. "I'm sorry, but we have to share the room, or we'll have a hell of a lot of explaining to do. It'll hurt my mother just as much as it would have hurt your grandmother to tell her the truth about our marriage."

"We can't sleep in the same bed."

He stood and crossed the room to take the letter from her and toss it on a table. He put his hands on her waist, and she wriggled away from him, stepping back and placing her hands on her hips. Her green eyes held pinpoints of fire, and he knew he was in for a battle.

"Don't you try to sweet-talk me, Josh Brand! Or kiss me into giving in to you! There's no way I'm getting into the same bed with you!"

"Is that right? If I stay way over on my side and

you stay way over on yours, what on earth would it hurt?''

''Dammit,'' she snapped. ''You know how susceptible I am to you—''

''No, I didn't know that,'' he said, his curiosity soaring along with his pulse. ''You always say no to me.''

''I don't say no fast enough! Look at me!'' She waved her hand at her wrinkled dress.

''I'm looking, and the view is mighty nice,'' he drawled. He wanted to peel away the sundress, to let his hands and mouth move over her bare skin. Just how much was she attracted to him? Was there any chance she would opt to stay at the ranch and forget law school? The idea intrigued him and made his pulse jump another notch. What if she would stay with Elizabeth and him? There was only one way to find the answer.

''Mattie, would you want to make this marriage real and forget law school?'' he asked and held his breath.

Her eyes narrowed, and she inhaled deeply. Josh listened to the steady ticking of the grandfather clock in the hall while he waited. ''Do you love me?'' she asked quietly.

Startled by her blunt question, Josh answered with honesty. ''I like you.''

''That isn't what I asked. And don't lie.''

''I won't lie to you.'' He thought about the depth of his feelings for her. He knew that every second that ticked past was driving a wedge between them, and he was going to lose this woman, but he didn't know the answer. ''Mattie, it hasn't been a year since I lost

Lisa. I'm changing, I know that. You're becoming important to me.''

Mattie had her answer and walked away from him. ''Let's get back to the bedroom problem.''

''Mattie, maybe if we tried to make this a real marriage, both of us would fall in love.''

She caught her lower lip with her teeth, then stared at him, and he wondered what was going through her thoughts. Slowly she shook her head. ''Or only one of us might fall in love, and the other one would get hurt badly.''

''Since when did you stop taking risks?'' he asked quietly, still searching his own feelings, fully aware he wanted her with an urgency that was beginning to demolish rational thought. At the same time, he wanted her companionship almost as badly as he wanted her body. *Was* he falling in love? The idea shocked him. A month ago he would have said it was impossible for him to love again.

''Josh, I have to give your questions some thought. And you should give them more thought, too.''

He nodded, thinking about a real marriage with Mattie. She had to be the one to make up her mind to stay. Never again would he push a woman into staying on the ranch. Memories of Lisa plagued him, coming as they often did without warning. Remembering her now, he hurt and felt the loss. Mattie was right. They shouldn't rush into anything.

He stared at her while he thought about his past and future. ''We better solve the problem at hand. Staying in the same room at Mom's won't be a dilemma. Knowing Mom, it'll be a king-size bed, and we'll have an ocean between us.''

"I still won't know how to socialize. I don't have the clothes, and I can't share a bed with you."

"You know how to socialize just fine, and we'll get you some dresses before we go. Mattie, Elizabeth's grandmother wants to see her grandchild. I'll sleep on the floor if necessary."

They stared at each other, and he felt the tug of wills, but beneath that, he kept wondering about their conversation. What would she have done if he had said he loved her? How strong were his feelings becoming for her?

She threw up her hands and headed toward the door. "All right. We'll go. I'll write your mother. Good night, Josh." She sailed out the door and he stared after her. She was in a huff, angry about the trip, but was there a chance *she* was falling in love with him? Rubbing the back of his neck, he turned out the lights and went outside to watch the lightning that was closer now.

For the rest of the week, Mattie drifted through the hours, either giving her attention to Elizabeth or thinking about her conversation with Josh. She'd lost sleep while she sat in the darkness and considered Josh's questions—just as she was doing now.

Maybe if we tried to make this a real marriage, both of us would fall in love. Her heart thudded every time she thought about his suggestion, remembering his solemn bass voice as he'd spoken. She wanted to toss aside the law books and tell him she wanted a real marriage, but that it was too soon. Only a few months before he had told her about nannies coming on to him and how he would never love again. What he was feeling now was physical attraction, she reminded herself again.

You're becoming important to me.

How important? She couldn't imagine Josh ready for another deep commitment. Too many times she had caught him with tears in his eyes or a sad expression, when she knew he was remembering Lisa.

And *she* didn't want to be hurt. How easily they could live together for a time, and then Josh really mend and fall in love with someone else. Or realize she was merely someone he physically craved and nothing more. She was not the type of woman a man like Josh would fall in love with, and all her wishful thinking wouldn't change the truth.

She flopped back in bed, staring at the moonlit night. She had better pursue law or get ready for a giant heartbreak.

On Monday Mattie drove to Austin and took the LSAT. That night at dinner, looking solemn, Josh asked her about it, then it wasn't mentioned again even though they sat together talking long into the night.

On Friday afternoon two weeks later Mattie heard a truck rumble up the drive to the house. Looking through the window, she saw the mailman, Virgil Grant, driving his delivery truck. He parked, stepped out and carried an armload of boxes toward the house.

"Hi, Virgil," she said as she opened the front door and held Elizabeth in her arms.

"Hi, Mattie. Hi, Li'l Bit," he said, grinning at Elizabeth. "Here's some boxes came for you from Dallas. Delivery left them yesterday, but it was too late to get out here until today. There's more in the truck."

"What is all this?" she asked, seeing her name on the order.

"Stuff for you. Good rain we had, wasn't it?"

"Yes," she answered perfunctorily while she watched him get another stack of boxes and place them in the entryway.

"Steamy as a jungle today, but I don't care. Rather have the rain. This is still an all-time record dry summer," Virgil said, rambling on. "Sign here. Li'l Bit, you're cute as a bug's ear. Ain't she growing like a weed?"

"She changes every week," Mattie said, handing him back his clipboard. He tore off a receipt and gave it to her.

"Thanks. Tell Josh hi."

Closing the door, she set Elizabeth down on the floor. "What on earth is all this?" she said, looking at long boxes, reading the store names. She opened one, lifted out a straight black dress and held it up in front of her. "My word! Elizabeth, your father doesn't know how to do things in a simple way."

She opened two more boxes and then closed them neatly, leaving them stacked where they were while she picked up Elizabeth to carry her to her room for her nap.

Later, Mattie saw Josh crossing the yard from the barn with his purposeful long stride. Even in dusty jeans and a T-shirt, he still looked handsome. He was a confident man who was full of vitality, and she suspected her remarks about his extravagance would fall on deaf ears. She waited for him to come through the kitchen door.

"Hi, Mattie. How was your day?" he asked, throwing his hat onto a peg. "It's hot out there. I think even hotter after the rain we had."

"Josh, all those dresses that you ordered were delivered."

He crossed to the fridge to get a cold beer. "Oh, yeah. Send back what you don't want. I don't care if you keep them all."

"Josh, there are twelve boxes in there."

He turned to look at her as he lowered the bottle and wiped his mouth. "You sound a little miffed. We can order more."

She threw up her hands in exasperation. "I don't need twelve dresses! One will do."

"Okay, after Elizabeth goes to bed, try them on and we'll pick out one or two."

"*I'll* select one."

"No. I know what Mom's parties are like. You try them on, and I'll help you select some."

Disconcerted, Mattie turned back to tearing bits of lettuce apart for salad, knowing she was losing another argument to him. Yet what he said made sense. What bothered her was the thought of modeling the dresses for him. She knew she would feel out of her element, uncertain and disturbed beneath his full scrutiny.

"You're really attacking that lettuce," he remarked near her shoulder, and she took a deep breath. His breath held the tint of beer, and he smelled dusty, slightly sweaty, yet she tingled with awareness. She could feel the heat from his body, feel a pull of tension that she experienced every time she was around him.

"It just seems a terrible extravagance—"

"We can send all but a couple back," he answered

lightly. "I'm going to shower. Want to come scrub my back?"

Startled, she looked up. He grinned and winked at her. "Gotcha, didn't I?" He turned and left the room, chuckling softly to himself, while she glared at his back and fought taunting images of him in the shower.

She tore at the crisp leaves of romaine without seeing them. Josh was definitely changing. He was more easygoing, always teasing her now. He wasn't as steeped in grief, seemed to notice her much more—and all of it made him more irresistible than ever. Yet she had asked him if he loved her and his answer was as obvious as if he had spoken the word *no* aloud. He said he liked her. That she was becoming important to him. In the short time since they'd been married, their relationship had changed. Would it continue to change? Was there a possibility he might love again?

How many times was she going to ask herself that question, she thought with annoyance. Minutes later, without realizing it, she stared at the yard while she wondered about Josh. She felt certain he would love again someday—he was too appealing and virile to remain single. But she couldn't fit herself into that picture. She could imagine him with some beautiful, sophisticated woman like his first wife.

Mattie dried her hands and checked on the baking chick en breasts, trying to focus on dinner and control her wayward thoughts about Josh.

Later that night, after Elizabeth had fallen asleep, Mattie went to her room and opened a box, removing a dress. It was a short black crepe, and she felt ridiculous going into the family room to model it for Josh. She was barefoot, her hair still in a pigtail. Tossing her braid over her shoulder, she entered the room. "Josh, why don't you tell me what type of dress I need. I feel ridiculous traipsing out here and I can't wear this. It's too short."

His expression was solemn as he stood and crossed the room to her. "Humor me and try them on. When you get to Chicago, you'll be thankful to have more than one dress. You don't know my mom."

Mattie groaned and closed her eyes, throwing her head back. "I'll embarrass you."

"Never," he said quietly, and she looked at him, startled by his solemn tone of voice. He moved closer, running his fingers along her hip. "You look beautiful. Standing here barefoot and in a pigtail, you're gorgeous. And that dress isn't one inch too short. Keep it, Mattie. Go try on another. I'll wait in my room, and you won't have as far to go back and forth."

"Why couldn't you have come into my life a long time ago?" she asked softly. She turned and rushed down the hall before he could answer. Her heart thudded while his words whirled in her mind. He thought she was gorgeous! Beautiful! He was tall enough that he didn't see her as a beanpole or giant. She closed the door to her room and looked at her image in the mirror. The dress was terribly short, but if Josh wanted her to keep it, she would.

The next box contained a red crepe with black velvet trim that molded to her body in plain lines. She saw the light on in his bedroom and entered to find him at his desk, writing in a ledger.

"How's this?"

He threw down his pen and swung around to look

at her slowly and deliberately in a study that made her tingle from head to toe.

"Perfect," he said. "Keep it."

"Josh, these dresses don't have the price tags on them."

"I told them to take the price tags off. We can afford those dresses. If you want to keep all of them, you can."

"Maybe you can afford them, but I can't!"

"You're not paying for them. I am, so forget the price."

"That really isn't good judgment."

He stood, then crossed the room to place his hands on her shoulders. "You're a wonderful woman, and we can ride all day and work cattle and horses and take care of Elizabeth without one tiny little argument. But when we get on personal grounds, everything is a tug-of-war."

"That you win too often."

"We can afford these dresses, Mattie. You don't cost much, you know. Before you became full-time mommy to Elizabeth, you rode and worked like one of the men. I figure you've earned this wardrobe."

"Maybe you should be the one to go into law." She shrugged and returned to her room. She tried on two more black dresses, a navy dress and a beige linen suit. When she returned to her room and opened the next box, she stared a moment, then lifted out a red leather miniskirt and red leather vest. Flinging them back into the box, she glanced over her shoulder, glaring in the direction of his room.

"Josh Brand, never in your lifetime!" she snapped as she opened another box with a pale yellow linen dress. She stepped into it, buttoning the back until she couldn't reach the buttons in the middle. Knowing most of the buttons were fastened, she went to his room.

"Here's the next one."

"Hey, that looks good. Keep it, too. Turn around."

"It's not buttoned. And I don't need all these dresses."

"Yes, you will. Mom will take you to lunch and shopping. Someone will have a tea. We'll have parties at night. I can button your dress—"

"No, you don't!" she snapped and left quickly, hurrying to her room.

She looked at the dresses hanging around the room and spread on the bed and thought about Josh. *Maybe if we tried to make this a real marriage, both of us would fall in love.*

You're becoming important to me.

Since when did you stop taking risks?

The words tormented her and sounded as if he were at her elbow whispering them instead of them whirling in her thoughts. When it came to love, she was inexperienced and vulnerable. But was Josh right? Should she take some risks? How many other times in her life had she stepped right in and taken risks? Too many to count. Yet with the man she truly loved, she was sitting back, terrified to risk her heart.

She was twenty-eight and had never been made love to, never given her body to a man. And her *husband* was sitting down the hall. He had already changed his attitude toward her a great deal. He said he liked her— how much deeper could it go?

She looked at the silly leather skirt while his words rushed at her. *Since when did you stop taking risks?*

Her heart began to pound as she stared at her image in the mirror. She didn't belong in a leather miniskirt any more than she belonged in Josh Brand's arms, yet he was the one who'd made the suggestion. And she was married to the man.

She shook her head and crossed the room to put the skirt back into the box. Tissue paper rustled as she folded the soft leather.

Since when did you stop taking risks? So she would get her heart broken. Wouldn't Josh and Elizabeth be worth the risk?

On impulse, Mattie squared her shoulders and yanked up the tiny leather vest along with the skirt.

She glanced at herself in the mirror and held the skirt in front of her. Lifting her chin, she tossed the skirt on the bed and began to unplait her braid. "All right, you asked for it," she mumbled as her fingers flew through her hair, combing out strands. Picking up her brush, she pulled it through her hair, brushing vigorously for the next five minutes.

She stripped to her lacy bra and panties, pulled on hose, and stepped into black high-heeled pumps. She stepped into the tiny red skirt, then zipped it and buttoned the waist. Next she pulled on the vest and buttoned it. She fastened gold earrings in her ears and put on mascara and blush. Finally she dabbed on her rose perfume. Stepping back, she studied herself in the mirror.

"I look ridiculous," she said quietly, feeling as if she were looking at a stranger. She wore more makeup than ever before in her life. The tiny skirt clung to her, and the vest left her arms bare and showed the beginning of curves. If she raised her arms, her midriff was bared. She felt as if she were staring at a total stranger.

"I don't know how to do this," she said. She shrugged. "You asked for this, Josh."

With her heart hammering, she went down the hall and stepped inside his room. "There's no way you really can expect me to wear this to a party of your mother's," she said, facing him with her hand on her hip.

Josh was pulling off his boots and as he turned, his gaze raked over her.

"Sweet Alice," he said, his breath coming out in a long rush. The appreciative stares she had received all evening were gone. Instead he looked dazed.

"Where *did* you expect me to wear this?" she asked, her voice lowering and becoming breathless.

Eight

With his dark gaze holding her mesmerized, Josh crossed the room and took her hand, pulling her with him to stand in front of the floor-to-ceiling mirror. He moved behind her, his hands on her arms while he leaned down to speak softly in her ear. "Look at yourself, Mattie. You can't ever doubt how sexy or how beautiful you look," he said in a husky voice.

She had no interest in looking at herself in the mirror, but instead watched him. He turned her to face him and placed his hands on her hips. In the midnight of his eyes, she saw his desire.

"Lady, you are all woman. Seductive, beautiful. And as long as I'm your husband, you won't wear that outfit anywhere outside this house." He stared at her as if probing for answers to unspoken questions. "Why did you decide to wear it now?"

"You bought it for me to wear. I guessed you wanted to see me in it," she answered, thinking about how he made her feel so very good, like a woman.

"So you did this for me?" he asked, his voice dropping to a husky rasp. "Ah, Mattie," he said softly with a warmth that caused her to tremble. His gaze went to her mouth. Her pulse raced, and her breasts tightened as her body responded to him without a stroke of his hand.

She was taking chances with her heart, with her future. Had she acted too impulsively? When she looked into his dark eyes, she knew her answer. She had found more happiness with Josh than she had ever known before in her life. She was married to him—a paper marriage—but was there a chance to make it real?

And even if he never loved her, Mattie knew she would have these moments with him to remember and treasure, something to hold forever.

He wrapped his arms around her tightly, pulling her to him as he bent his head to kiss her. "So beautiful," he whispered before his mouth covered hers and he kissed her long and hard.

Her pulse drummed, racing too fast as she slipped her arms around his neck. She pressed against him and returned his kisses.

In spite of his arms holding her tightly and his assertions that she looked pretty, old uncertainties haunted her. She wasn't sophisticated or experienced. When it came to love, she was as green as a very young girl, while the man holding her was just the opposite.

Josh pushed her away slightly, his hands twisting

free the brass buttons of the vest. He shoved it off her shoulders as he kissed her. In seconds her bra followed, the air cool on her bare flesh.

She could feel the tremble in his hands, see the need in his expression, and it astounded her that he could want her to such an extent. She felt his fingers at the zipper of her skirt.

The leather skirt fell around her ankles. He stepped back, his eyes burning with desire as he looked at her. His shaking hands cupped her breasts and he inhaled, his chest expanding. He bent his head, his tongue circling a nipple.

Sensations rippled in her; need moved her hips with urgency. Her fears vanished as she clung to his strong shoulders, closing her eyes, hearing dimly the moan that must be her own. He took her nipple into his mouth, teasing so lightly with his teeth and tongue, driving her beyond thought. She knew she wanted his loving, wanted to know him intimately. And in the deep recesses of her heart, she knew she wanted to bind this man to her as she was already bound to him.

She stepped out of the skirt that was in a heap around her ankles while Josh knelt in front of her. He hooked his fingers in the waist of her pantyhose and panties, peeling them away as he trailed kisses of fire across her flat stomach and to her inner thighs. His hands were splayed on her hips and then he trailed his hands around her, skimming over her buttocks, down her thighs.

With his eyes devouring her, he stood. His arms wrapped around her, crushing her to him as he kissed her hard. She could barely get her breath, yet it was glorious to be held in his strong arms, enclosed so tightly as if she were vital to him. For moments she returned his kisses and then she tugged at his T-shirt, wanting to feel his flesh against hers.

Josh yanked off his shirt and tossed it aside. He unbuckled his belt and jeans and stepped out of them. She touched his chest, and her gaze locked on his magnificent body. She ran her hands over his broad chest, down to his slender hips. Her fingers brushed lightly over his manhood. He shed his briefs and she wrapped her fingers around his shaft, hearing his gasp for breath as she stroked him.

She could feel a blush burn her throat and face as she stroked him brazenly, yet she wanted him with a need that consumed her. She wanted to make up for lost time and unfulfilled longings.

His body was bronze, even darker above the waist where he had worked shirtless in the sun. His body rippled with muscles and was lean and hard. She loved him and she might as well face the fact, but she knew she couldn't tell him until he made a declaration. She would never want him to feel trapped.

She kissed him, showering kisses across his chest, her hands exploring his body, learning the flat planes, the ridges of muscle, the protrusion of his hip bones, his hard thighs. She knelt, kissing him, closing her fingers around his rigid shaft as she stroked and kissed.

Dazed, Josh yielded to her loving, feeling as if he would explode with need. Mattie was as direct in her loving as she was in everything else, and she was driving him to a brink where his control would shatter. He groaned, winding his fingers in her thick, silky hair, wanting to shove her to the floor and take her hard and fast, to consume the warmth and passion she would give.

Yet he knew he had to curb his desire and give her time. Above all else, this should be the night for restraint.

Beneath the scalding desire, he was still stunned. He would remember forever looking up and seeing her standing across the room in the tight red miniskirt and vest. She would stop traffic on main street in Dallas, and yet he knew the woman had little confidence in her own femininity. As a lover, she was about to turn him to cinders.

Knowing he was losing control, he reached for her and pulled her up.

Josh's fingers locked on Mattie's arms, and he lifted her to her feet. He swung her into his embrace, his body warm and hard against hers. She clung to him, gazing back at him, relishing his holding her and his strong arms encircling her. Her body ached with a need she had never really experienced before. Should she warn him of her virginity? Would he be annoyed?

He carried her to his bed. With a sweep of his arm he ripped back the covers and lowered her to the cool navy sheet, coming down over her to wind his fingers in her hair and stare at her.

"I want you," he said in a husky voice, bending his head to kiss her. His tongue thrust into her mouth in a rhythm that was a reminder of a deeper joining of their bodies. His hands stroked, sliding down her side and over the curve of her hip while she arched against him and returned his kisses.

Josh shifted, trailing kisses down to her breasts and then moving lower, watching her as he kissed the inside of her thigh and his fingers delved in her secret places. Her green eyes glowed with desire. She arched against his hand until he found her feminine bud and began another rhythmic stroking that drove her wild.

Uncertainty vanished and a raging need built as she moved and wound her fingers in his hair. And then his tongue was where his fingers had been and she felt as if she would splinter into fragments. "Josh!"

"I want you to want me," he whispered. "I want those long legs of yours holding me."

She couldn't answer him. Her body was wracked with need, her hips thrusting as she felt the tension coil within her. She cried out when the shattering release came, only it made her want more and she scrambled up, sliding her arms around his neck and pulling him over her.

"Now, Josh," she whispered, and he inhaled, winding his fingers in her hair. He shifted between her thighs, then abruptly rose to his knees.

"Are you on the Pill, Mattie?"

"No. I don't have any protection."

He reached across her to open a drawer in the bedside table and removed a packet. As he started to slide on the thin sheath, she reached out to help, her fingers playing over him, sliding down between his legs to cup him. He groaned and pushed her to the bed, moving closer between her thighs.

He was poised over her, virile, aroused, incredibly handsome. She felt as if her body were swelling, thrusting toward him with an ancient need that would mirror what she had already given from her heart.

He moved down over her, his mouth taking hers and she closed her eyes, wrapping her legs around him, feeling the firm mounds of his buttocks against her legs. She wanted to enclose him with her body, envelope him with her love.

He entered her and paused, and she thought she would faint with the need that burned low in her body. Her breasts were taut, her body aching, her hips arching against him. All her awareness was of their bodies, of Josh's body one with hers.

"Josh, please," she whispered.

"Please what?" he asked, and her eyes flew open to find him watching her. "I want to hear you say it."

"I want you. You know I want you."

Josh's heart thudded. His body was drenched in sweat, and he was fighting to control himself and hold back. She was moving against him, only the tip of his shaft enveloped in her softness. He thrust slowly then, with a deliberateness that was making him shake and burn.

He was surprised when he felt the virgin barrier. He looked at her, saw her white teeth biting her lip. Perspiration dotted her brow, and her eyes were closed, but when he paused, she looked up at him.

"Mattie—" He couldn't talk. He kissed her, wishing he could keep her from feeling any pain, easing in and withdrawing, trying to take her to a point where she would want him desperately.

She moaned and arched against him, her fingers squeezing his buttocks. Her legs tightened around him, and he knew he had held back as long as he could.

He thrust, entering her fully, taking her cry in his kisses as they moved together.

Sensations flooded Mattie, and her world consisted of the powerful man in her arms as she rocked with him and felt the tension build. White fire danced behind her eyelids and a roaring in her ears shut out all other sounds. Dimly she heard a cry and realized it was her own while her hands raked over Josh's strong back. For now, he was hers and they were one.

She arched, the momentary pain transforming into ecstasy and urgency until she crashed over a brink.

"Mattie!" Josh's cry was harsh. His powerful body shuddered with release, and she tightened her arms and legs around him while she was carried to another brink and felt release burst deep within her.

She gasped for breath. Slowly the world steadied and settled, and thought returned. She stroked his smooth back, knowing that whatever the future held, she would have this night to treasure forever.

Josh's arms were under her, his weight heavy now, yet she relished holding him. She turned her head to find him watching her, and then he leaned the few inches and kissed her as long and passionately as he had before their lovemaking.

She shifted away slightly to look at him, running her finger along his cheek, pushing his hair away from his face. His long black hair was disheveled, giving him a wild, savage look until she gazed in his eyes and saw the incredible warmth there. He was damp with sweat and looking at her with such tenderness she felt she would melt.

"Are you hurt?"

"What do you think?" she asked, knowing she would be sore, but not caring. "Did I act like I hurt?"

"Hardly." He leaned down to kiss her throat, trailing kisses to her mouth. "So special, Mattie."

She wasn't certain she heard correctly, but she

didn't care. She was more aware of his kisses than his conversation, and she turned her head to kiss him deeply. His arms tightened around her, and she felt him growing hard again deep within her. Surprised, she looked up at him, leaning back to study him.

"You don't have any idea how much you excite me," he said quietly. "I haven't slept at night for weeks, Mattie. And I know damned well I won't sleep tonight. Not as long as you'll let me hold you in my arms."

Her heart thudded with his words and with the look of longing in his eyes. She had expected to see satisfaction, to find him satiated and that his interest in her would have lessened after their lovemaking. Instead, he was looking at her with more longing than before, and she could feel the changes in him within her, his shaft thickening, pushing against her and exciting her all over again.

"I could take you right now. I want to and you know it," he said in a husky voice. "Instead—" He shifted, moving away from her and stepping off the bed. He lifted her into his arms and headed toward the bathroom. "We're going to shower and start all over. And this time I'll be able to go slower, to love you until you faint."

"You almost did before."

"This time will be more for you," he said, turning on the water and then stepping beneath the hot spray. Water splashed over her, and she ran her hands across his broad shoulders.

"Let me take care of necessities and keep you protected," he said. He stepped out of the shower, leaving her a moment while he closed the shower door. In seconds he was back and she inhaled at the sight of his virile, nude body. Desire was a hot flame burning low in her body, crawling through her veins. She wondered if she should feel embarrassed. Instead, it was heavenly to be with him, to have him move about casually with her, to feel closer to him, more intimate with him than with any other person in her life.

"Josh," she whispered as she slid her hands over his strong, wet body, feeling his smooth skin. He stepped beneath the shower. The water spilled over him and he slicked back his raven hair, then his hands trailed over her body, cupped her breasts and their lovemaking began again.

It was morning before she dozed, and when she opened her eyes she found him propped on his elbow watching her. "Good morning."

"Don't you ever sleep?"

"Not this night." He held a lock of her hair and trailed it across her ear and over her cheek. "Will you move into my room, Mattie?"

She stared at him while she mulled it over. She wanted more from him; she wanted his love. If she moved into his room, would it make the hurt deeper when they parted? Or was there a chance it would bind them closer?

"I didn't exactly plan this out, Josh. You bought that silly skirt and vest and I put it on, but I didn't think too far in the future."

"I want you in here," he said solemnly. While she thought about the night, she gazed into his eyes that were so dark it was almost impossible to distinguish iris from pupil. His lashes were thick and long, a dark fringe framing his eyes. He was waiting patiently for her decision and a *yes* rose swiftly to her lips, but she held back to give thought to her answer. He had held her, loved her in so many ways, cried out her name. But not once had he declared his love.

At the same time, it didn't mean he wouldn't fall in love someday. She ran her fingers along his jaw and felt the slight bristles. "You don't have hair on your chest, yet you have a thick head of hair and you have to shave every day."

"Mixed genes. My white and Native American blood. I have enough white blood to have to do all that shaving. But don't change the topic. I want you in my bed. It was so damned good, Mattie. I feel alive for the first time in a long, long time."

She wrapped her arms around him, and he tightened his arms around her to hold her close. She could feel their hearts beating together, and she wondered about this strong, handsome man. Would he ever love her? Was she chasing rainbows and dreaming fantasies? Yet the night had been real, and if what he was saying was true, it had been special for him, too.

"I'll move my things today," she answered.

He shifted, turning his head to kiss her as conversation vanished.

She dozed later and woke to find him gone. Startled and wondering about Elizabeth, Mattie climbed out of bed and looked at the clock. It was seven-thirty. She stood, looking down at herself. She yanked a sheet off the bed, wrapped it around her and hurried out of the room. Maria only came in late afternoons, and Mattie expected Josh had already left to work. The only thing she could think of was that Elizabeth had slept late, but it was difficult to imagine. Elizabeth usually was up with the sun.

She hurried to the nursery to find it empty. Startled, Mattie rushed down the hall. "Elizabeth! Li'l Bit!"

"Down here, Mattie," came a masculine reply and she slowed. She entered the kitchen to find Josh feeding Elizabeth. The baby had oatmeal on her face and hands, and she smiled at Mattie.

"Mama!" She held out grubby hands.

"No way, sweetie," Mattie said, looking at Josh, whose frank appraisal made her aware of the sheet wrapped tightly around her.

He wore a fresh T-shirt and jeans, and desire streaked through her, hot and intense and startling.

"She was a good girl and slept late this morning. We tried not to wake you."

Mattie barely heard him. Her attention was on his chest and she was remembering the night and their lovemaking. She realized the room had become silent except for Elizabeth clattering a spoon.

Josh's eyes narrowed, and he inhaled deeply. "Mattie—"

She heard the husky note in his voice, saw the urgency in his eyes that she felt, yet Elizabeth was banging on her high chair and Mattie knew they had to get back into their routine. "I'll dress," she said hurriedly and fled down the hall.

She closed the door to her room and leaned against it, her heart hammering and her palms damp. She wanted him more than ever. It should be the other way around, she thought. She should feel satisfied, exhausted. Instead, one look at his strong, virile body, and she wanted his arms around her again.

She stared at herself, still amazed by the events of the night and the changes in her life. She looked the same as always, but she had changed in every other way. She was deeply and irrevocably in love with a man who might not ever love her in return. She was bound to Josh and Elizabeth, loving them both, wanting her life to be entwined forever with theirs. And she was a woman now. This morning she felt desirable, feminine—all because of Josh.

Not all her old uncertainties were gone, though. The trip to Chicago was a dark cloud on the horizon. She would be completely out of her element, and she might not be the woman Josh expected her to be. Mattie held up her long hair. She should make an appointment to get a stylish haircut. And make an appointment with a doctor to get birth control.

But right now the trip was days away, and for today she wasn't going to worry about it. Today she was going to play with Elizabeth and remember the night with Josh.

Later that morning, when she told Josh goodbye at the back door, he lingered, kissing her until they were both gasping for breath. "If we didn't have Elizabeth on our hands, I'd stay home from work today."

"But we do and you can't."

"I'll be home as early as possible. And I'll be thinking about you all day."

"You better think about what you're doing before a horse kicks you," she remarked.

He didn't laugh but stared at her solemnly. "It was good, Mattie. Really good."

Her heart thudded. His admission seemed another link in the chain that was slowly forging between them. "I think so, too," she said, wondering if the barrier of grief around him, that part of his heart that was locked away, was slowly opening to her.

He turned, and in long strides headed for the pickup parked near the barn.

The next three weeks were idyllic. But as the trip to Chicago drew near, Mattie began worrying about the visit. On the day before they were to leave for Chicago, she received the results of her LSAT. That night as Josh held her close, their bodies damp from loving, she told him, "I passed the LSAT."

He became still a moment, then raised up to look down at her. His features were impassive as he gave her a probing look. "So now that hurdle is out of your way."

Mattie stared at him, wanting him to urge her to forget law school, to tell her he wanted her to stay with him always.

Instead he leaned down to kiss her, a long, hungry kiss that made her forget law school or ever leaving his embrace.

On the following day they left for Chicago. With butterflies in her stomach, Mattie watched DFW airport recede below as the jet lifted, banked and headed north. She had a new shoulder-length haircut that Josh had protested about two seconds after he had complimented her. Since then she could count more than a dozen times when he had told her that he liked her hair long.

She had two suitcases filled with new clothing, and Josh's fingers were linked with hers, yet she couldn't stop the trepidation she felt. Too many times in the past she had been a social outcast, and she was terrified of facing Chicago society.

They landed in Chicago, where Sibyl met them, and in the next few whirlwind hours Mattie forgot her apprehension. She had asked Sibyl to make a hair appointment so she could get her hair washed and styled after their arrival. The appointment was made for the second day, and on their first night they had dinner at home with only Thornton and Sibyl. By ten o'clock they retired to their bedroom. The moment Josh closed the door, he slid his arm around her waist and pulled her to him.

"See, I told you we wouldn't have any difficulty sharing a bedroom," he said in a husky voice, while his fingers were at the back of her yellow linen dress.

One look in his dark eyes and any answer she might have had vanished from thought. She wound her arms around his neck, pressed against him and kissed him. His arms tightened, and in minutes the yellow dress was a heap around her ankles. Josh picked her up to carry her to the king-size bed.

Later, as Mattie lay sleeping in his arms, Josh smoothed her hair from her face. He ran his fingers lightly along her warm shoulder and slender arm. He felt lucky; his life was righting itself, the terrible pain of loss and the agony of grief beginning to recede to memories. He was alive again and he was damned lucky to have found Mattie. He was falling in love with this woman who was becoming incredibly special to him. He wanted her to stay forever on the ranch, but she had to make that decision herself. Never again would he push a woman to stay where she didn't want to be.

He lifted locks of her hair, thinking about the surprise of seeing it cut, realizing she was trying to fit into his mother's group of friends and look less like a country girl from Texas. He leaned forward to brush her temple lightly with a kiss. Would she want to stay on the ranch? Would she give up a lifelong dream of becoming a lawyer? Or was he going to love and lose again?

Only a few weeks earlier she had asked him if he loved her, and he hadn't given her an answer. Now he could give her an answer straight from his heart. At the first good moment, he intended to tell her. He was tempted to wake her now.

He should have told her tonight, but words vanished when she came eagerly into his arms. "I love you, Mattie," he whispered.

Her lashes were feathery against her pale skin, her silken hair spilling over her cheek and throat. The sheet was tucked beneath her arms, and as his gaze roamed down he caressed her arm. With deliberation he pushed the sheet lower so her breasts were bare. He marveled at her as he reacted to looking at her.

Mattie was so many contradictions, even physical ones. She was tall, a strong woman with great physical energy. At the same time, she was so incredibly soft, so feminine in moments of loving. Her skin was pale and delicate, her curves lush and enticing. She seemed a woman lacking confidence in her femininity, yet when she had appeared in the red leather skirt and vest, she was seductive and certain of herself.

His body tightened as he became aroused, wanting her. Forgetting thoughts of the future, he pushed the sheet away and slowly trailed his fingers across her breasts, watching her and waiting for her to stir. He leaned down to flick his tongue over her nipple, feeling the bud grow taut as Mattie moaned softly.

Josh shifted, trailing kisses on her smooth skin. She was warm, languid, and he knew in minutes her languor would transform to hot responses that would scald him. His hands played over her as she moaned again and shifted in a lazy, sensual stretch. Then her hands locked in his hair and she twisted around, pulling him to her, her green eyes stormy with desire.

Winding her arms tightly around him, Mattie kissed him. As he pushed her back down on the bed and moved over her, his pulse pounded. This time he didn't want to wait. He entered her hard and fast. Her long legs locked around him as she kissed him and moved with him and he was lost to passion.

Nine

"**D**oes my hair look all right?" Mattie asked. Josh paused in fastening the strip of rawhide behind his head to turn and look at her. She had changed, and with her new haircut and the slinky black dress she looked sophisticated, and tall enough to be an attention getter. His body clenched, heat suffusing him as he remembered how she had looked this morning when he'd first awakened and she was lying naked in his arms.

"You look gorgeous," he said in a husky voice. Mentally he stripped away the black dress, which left her arms bare and revealed her long, shapely legs. Her hair fell loose, turning under slightly just above her shoulders with short bangs framing her forehead. She looked so sexy he longed to have the party over and be back in this bedroom with her for the night. He glanced at his watch. "And if I thought we wouldn't be disturbed, I would haul you into my arms for some fast lovemaking." He pulled on his navy suit coat and straightened his tie.

"Indeed you won't!" she snapped, walking around him to lean forward and study herself intently in the mirror. "Josh, I can't do this!"

"Don't be ridiculous. It's just a dinner party. You look great," he said, studying her legs.

"I won't know what to say, and I feel like the country girl who will be seen as such a hick."

"Mom's from Clayton County. I was born there. Probably half the people who will be here tonight have some kind of rural background in their lives." Josh thought all her worries were unfounded, yet he knew to Mattie they were real. And he suspected she had had some terrible times growing up. He pushed his coat open, placing his hands on his hips as he watched her.

"Sometimes I almost want to take you to town in your red miniskirt and vest, just so you can watch those guys who called you names in high school come drooling after you. But I said *almost*. No way in hell will I give them a chance with you."

"That's ridiculous," she said offhandedly. "Right now, it's tonight I'm worried about. In these shoes I'm over six feet tall—something most men hate. This dress is short and my legs look impossibly long."

"Mattie, your legs are fabulous, and if guys stare—which they will—it's because they think you're gorgeous. These are not fifteen-year-old boys—this party will have only adults who may not even notice your height. Let's go kiss Elizabeth good-night, and then we'll join the party. Stop worrying.''

''That's so easy for you to say. You've been at ease in situations like this since you were a toddler.''

''You're stewing over nothing. You're not thirteen. You're grown, married, very intelligent and competent, and you'll be the best-looking and sexiest woman here, lady.''

''Oh, if only—''

''You'll see,'' he said, taking her hand. He frowned, looking at her again. Her hands were as cold as ice, and he felt a slight tremor. ''Mattie, relax.'' She stared at him solemnly, and he knew his words were in vain. ''If it'll be any consolation to you, I won't leave your side.''

Mattie gave him a faint, chilly smile and the uncertainty in her green eyes made him want to put his arm around her and stay at her side the whole evening.

''Come on. It won't be so dreadful. It's just friends of Mom's and Thornton's.''

They went to the nursery to kiss Elizabeth, then headed downstairs. As they approached the front room, voices were loud, the music from a string quartet barely audible over the din of people talking. His mother had planned this large buffet dinner party for over fifty friends. He knew it was a reception for the new bride and groom and to introduce both of them to their Chicago friends. He glanced at Mattie, whose chin was raised, a look of grim determination in her expression.

''There you are,'' Sibyl said, rushing forward to greet them. She wore a navy dress with white trim, and her eyes sparkled with delight. Josh knew his mother relished a party as much as Mattie enjoyed riding and ranching.

"Let me introduce you to everyone. Tom and Eunice just arrived and they've never met Josh, either."

Mattie's heart raced, and she felt stiff and ill at ease. As she moved around the room between Sibyl and Josh, she smiled at people, trying to get names firmly in mind, shaking hands with a senator and his wife, smiling at an artist, then moving to the next couple. For the first half hour Josh was at her side, sounding completely at ease, charming the ladies.

She felt tall, awkward, as uncomfortable as she had at parties in college or as a teen, but when no one singled her out, and Josh's arm stayed firmly around her waist, she began to relax. The people were warm and friendly, and as she stood listening to a group of people, her nerves calmed.

A waiter served white wine, and Mattie took a glass, listening while everyone discussed the coming football season. Talk changed from football to weather. "I hear you're having an unusually hot, dry summer," a tall brown-haired man said to Josh.

"We're going to set a record this year. Our rainfall is way below average. Our part of the state usually gets rain."

"Your mother said you're a rancher," Tim Colby remarked. Mattie had met Tim earlier and knew he was a former neighbor and longtime friend of Thornton's. "I just bought horses for the family. We're not horse people, though. We just want to ride with the kids. We're having the damnedest time with one of the horses. He's gentle and manageable until we leave the paddock. Damned animal just wants to stay home.

He doesn't want to get a hundred yards from the paddock. You ever heard of that?''

"My wife's the horse expert. Mattie?'' Josh said, glancing down at her.

"They have an old term for horses who don't want to leave home,'' she said, knowing full well Josh could have answered the man as easily as she could. "I've heard my father call them barn-sour horses. I never did understand the term. Barn sour sounds as if the horse doesn't want to stay in the barn when it's really the other way around.''

"It's nice to know it's not unique to this horse. Is there any cure? I don't like fighting with him every time we try to ride. And my family would leave me if I beat the stubborn cuss.''

Mattie smiled, feeling sure of herself. "You should be able to get him to lose the habit.''

"How's that?''

"When you leave the paddock and he starts to balk, keep him moving. Keep the reins loose and pressure him with your heels.''

"Why keep the reins loose?'' Tim Colby asked. "Seems like I won't have control.''

"If you don't keep the reins loose, he may begin to fight you more. He may start tossing his head. Make him move along, but don't direct him. You'll probably go in big circles. It'll take some working with a horse like that. Some horses are the same way about leaving a herd. They just want to stay with other animals or stay home in the barn.''

"You've owned horses like that?'' a broad-shouldered blond man standing beside her asked. She glanced at him, remembering Josh introducing them. Allen Anderson.

"Yes. With just a little effort some horses get over wanting to stay in the barn. Some you have to work with quite a while." She turned back to Tim Colby. "If it's a young horse or a sensitive one, pressure from your heels or legs will keep him moving. If you keep him going, gradually he'll decide staying at the paddock isn't worth the struggle."

"This is a wonderful animal as long as he's in the paddock," Harriet Colby said. "Our children adore this horse, so we can't get rid of him."

"Is he young?"

"He's two. Now Tim's horse—that's the one I can't ride!" Harriet said laughing.

"When you're through riding, don't unsaddle him right away," Mattie added. "This will lower his eagerness to return to the paddock so quickly."

"Maybe now I can get my money's worth out of that horse," Tim Colby said.

As Mattie discussed horses, she realized Josh had moved away. She saw him with another group of people, and he glanced at her as he sipped his drink. He lifted his glass in a slight salute to her and winked. She smiled at him.

She continued answering questions and talking about horses, barely noticing when dinner was announced. As Allen took her arm, she glanced around to see Josh still standing across the room. His back was turned and he was talking to two men. He was taller than the rest of the crowd and it was easy to spot his dark head.

"You're newlyweds, aren't you?" Allen asked, drawing her attention back to him.

"Yes. We married in April," she replied, gazing into his blue eyes.

"So you're probably not interested in meeting me for lunch this week?"

She smiled as she shook her head. "Thanks, but no."

"I can show you around Chicago while Josh is busy doing whatever he does when he's here."

"Thanks, but I think my mother-in-law has our time planned."

The dining room table was laden with brisket, roast duck, pale slices of chicken breasts in mushroom and caper sauce, steaming vegetables and golden dinner rolls. Candles flickered in silver candelabra, reflecting in the crystal goblets and serving bowls. People served themselves in a buffet line and spread over the house to eat at tables that had been set up.

As soon as they were seated at a table for eight, Allen was at her side and a couple named Reider sat across from them. "We hear you know horses. I'm Jess Reider," the blond man announced. "This is my wife, Kate."

In minutes Mattie was in another horse conversation, and she lost track of time, feeling as much at home as if she had been in Texas. By the time Josh came to join them, Mattie's table was filled with guests, and he moved on to another table.

An hour after dinner Josh stood across the room and idly sipped a glass of wine while he watched her. She stood in a group of men who were hanging on her every word. Why had the woman worried? She was the hit of the party, and if she didn't have his wedding ring on her finger, he would bet that she would have dates lined up for the rest of the week. She looked poised, radiant, beautiful, and he felt a pain around his heart.

She had taken to these people like a flower turning to sunshine. Mattie should have her chance in the world. She had always dreamed of law school and her application had been accepted. She was intelligent and outgoing. He couldn't try to hold her on the ranch. She belonged with people, doing things besides being isolated on a ranch as a nanny and a housewife and riding like a cowhand day after day.

He moved through French doors and went outside on the terrace, walking down through the garden where he could be alone. He was the one who belonged on the ranch. He liked the solitude, the simpler life in so many ways. It was tough, but challenging, and it was for him. It was all he knew, all he was trained for. And he loved it. But his beautiful wife should be set free.

Hurting, he crossed the estate grounds and walked down toward the pond, looking at its shimmering smooth surface and thinking about Mattie and how she looked tonight. In so many ways she seemed like a different person than the neighboring rancher to whom he had proposed a marriage of convenience.

It had been so convenient for him, but she was right. She had warned him he would be sorry. She had warned him he would fall in love. At the time, he hadn't thought it was possible.

Needing to do something physical, he picked up a flat stone and sent it skipping over the water. He watched it bounce and bounce and sink, leaving widening circles of ripples in its wake.

He wanted to go back into the party, get his wife and daughter and go home to Texas. He wanted Mattie in his arms and in his bed and in his life.

"Hellfire," he said softly, realizing he should have listened to her warnings. He was going to get hurt badly again, but he knew he had to let Mattie go. It was his own damned fault. All of this was his doing, and he had known from the first that a sham marriage wasn't fair to her.

He turned and strode back to the house, stepping inside, and standing near the door to watch Mattie. She fairly glowed with happiness, and he suspected her qualms about social engagements would end tonight.

"Hey, Josh," Ed Burnes called, and Josh turned to join Thornton's speechwriter and the group of people he accompanied.

While Mattie stood in a cluster of guests, she felt an invisible tug and glanced over her shoulder. Looking so darkly handsome, Josh was across the room in another group of guests with his steady, smoldering gaze on her. In his dark suit and crisp white shirt, he was the most handsome man in the room. But there was also a streak of wildness about his appearance that none of the other men had. His skin was darker from working outside, and even in a party, while he stood visiting with others, he exuded a raw vitality.

Now as he stared back at her, his somber expression made her wonder what he was thinking. He winked, a special little signal for her alone, and she forgot the party and the room filled with people. She winked in return, wishing the party were over and she was upstairs, alone with Josh. When he turned his head and spoke to someone, she guessed the person had asked him a question.

"I envy him," a deep voice said beside her, and she looked around to find Allen Anderson moving close to her side. He shifted in front of her, cutting off the group of people she had been standing with.

"I'm very much married," she said firmly, and he shrugged.

"I'm convinced. All anyone has to do is see you two look at each other. And if looks could kill, the few I've received from your devoted husband would have done the job. But if only—"

"Don't monopolize the lady," a man said lightly, and she turned to see one of the guests she had met earlier. "Sibyl tells me you've won trophies for barrel racing. Is that right?"

"Yes," Mattie answered, trying to recall the man's name. In minutes she was surrounded by a group again who wanted to hear about her rodeo experiences.

It was one o'clock before the party broke up. As the door closed after the last guest, Sibyl turned to them. "Everyone adored the two of you. We're going to have the most fun this week."

"You mean everyone adored my lovely wife," Josh said, sliding his arm around her waist and gazing at her solemnly.

"The party was wonderful fun," Mattie said. "I really enjoyed it."

"We'll have a wonderful time tomorrow, too," Sibyl stated.

"See you in the morning, Mom." Josh brushed her cheek with a kiss. "Night, Thornton."

"It was a great party," Thornton said, looking up at his tall stepson. "Good night, you two."

Wanting his wife with a heat that had built through the night, Josh draped his arm across Mattie's shoulders. He walked in silence back to their room, listening to Mattie talk about people she had met. Excitement bubbled in her, and Josh wanted all that vitality turned into passion. He felt like running to their room to get her alone as quickly as possible. More than ever, he wanted her. And while she chattered to him about the party, he barely heard a word she said while erotic fantasies played in his mind. He watched the slight swing of her breasts as she walked beside him. He tightened his arm across her shoulders and pulled her closer against his side.

Mattie glanced up at Josh. "You were right. They were all so nice."

"Yeah. Especially Allen Anderson. I wanted to punch him out. And I would have if he had taken you off alone."

Mattie laughed. "He was friendly."

"Yeah. I could tell his friendly intentions by the way he looked at you. He wanted to devour you." Josh glanced down at her, mentally stripping away the black dress, envisioning Mattie's lush naked body.

"You were right about the party. I shouldn't have worried. Everyone was so nice, and a lot of them were interested in some of the same things we are."

Josh closed the bedroom door and turned her to face him, sliding his arms around her waist. She gazed into unfathomable dark eyes. His expression was solemn, and he had been so quiet. "What's wrong?" she asked.

As he studied her in silence, Mattie began to get a strong feeling that something was terribly awry. The shuttered look that he'd had when she first met him had come back. His arms tightened around her, and he leaned down to kiss her passionately as if he hadn't kissed her in weeks. His tongue went deeply into her mouth, and then he sucked her tongue into his mouth and bit gently as if he were taking every inch of her that he could.

Her heart thudded, and she wound her arms around his neck, returning his kisses while her body responded instantly to him. She forgot her suspicions that something was wrong. She moved closer to him, pressing her hips against his, wanting to feel the solid hardness of him from chest to thigh.

Something had given an added urgency to his lovemaking. She didn't know what, but she relished the results because she could feel that he wanted her more than ever before.

Even as he held her tightly in his arms, Josh knew he was losing her. He had to let her go, but he wanted her desperately. He leaned back against the door, spread his legs and pulled her up against his body, feeling her soft contours press against him. She smelled like flowers and tasted hot and sweet. He was hard with need and longing.

He slid his hands across her shoulders, found the zipper of her dress and slowly tugged it down her back. He pushed the dress away and let it fall around her feet. Clothing became aggravating barriers. He wanted her body against his. Tonight she was his, and he would not think about tomorrow and what was to come and what he had to do.

"You're wonderful, Mattie," he whispered, wanting to add that he loved her, yet knowing he shouldn't. He had bound her in a fake marriage, and he never should have. Now he would not hold her with a love that might cost her her dreams. Yet to the depths of his being, he wanted her love. He had loved Lisa, and at the time he'd thought it was an everlasting, total love, but with Lisa he had never had what he had found with Mattie. He and Mattie were one in so many ways. She was a peer whose opinion he respected. She was a companion whose company was a delight. She was a lover who made the nights rapture and kept him in a constant state of arousal.

He groaned, tightening his arms around her. "Ah, woman," he said in a husky voice. "My woman," he stated fiercely, wishing it were true. He slid his hands down to cup her bottom and pull her up more tightly against him. His hard shaft was between them, and her hips ground against him, making him shake with desire.

He felt her hands pushing between them, tugging at his shirt, and he released her slightly while she pulled his shirt out of his trousers. Her eyes were half-closed, the green depths burning with fires that mirrored his feelings. Her fingers fluttered and stroked his chest, and electricity zinged from her touch to his groin.

He framed her face, his fingers wound in her hair as he tilted her head to look into her eyes. "I want you, Mattie." His voice was rough with passion, shaken by emotion. He kissed her hard, his hands ripping away the last of her underwear.

Mattie could sense the difference in him. There was a wild urgency to his kisses. He was rough, holding her more tightly than usual. To her surprise it heightened her excitement to know that he wanted her so desperately. She would never become accustomed to the effect she had on him.

He looked at her with such hunger and need that she felt a burning ache to give to him. Her hips twisted against his, an urgency building in her that began to match his.

He raised his head and yanked off his clothing, and she wondered if his body would always be a breathtaking marvel to her.

"Mattie, come here," he whispered, pulling her down on the thick carpet. Mattie's pulse pounded with eagerness. Exhilaration from the evening heightened her responses while Josh's urgency fanned the flames within her. She pushed him to his back, moving over him, and his hands held her hips, settling her on him. His shaft was thick, easing into her and filling her. Her cry was a faint sound over the roaring in her ears while her hips moved rhythmically. She felt complete with him, a miracle each time they united, something so special it was worth all the long, lonely years of waiting.

As he entered her and she moved her hips, he caressed her and trailed his fingers between her legs. She closed her eyes, catching her lower lip with her teeth while her head thrashed and her hair flew across her shoulders.

With a harsh sound Josh shifted and rolled her over, moving on top of her, thrusting in her wildly. She clung to him, her legs locked around his waist, the rising ardor carrying them on a tide that shut out everything else.

"Mattie, love!"

The words Josh cried out were dim, his voice hoarse, words that barely registered in Mattie's mind in the midst of passion. Release burst within her while Josh still moved, his body thrusting with his release. Her pulse roared as rapture enveloped her. Her breathing slowly returned to normal. When her heartbeat slowed, she opened her eyes to find him watching her. He bent his head to kiss her as hungrily as if they had never made love.

He carried her to bed, holding her tightly in his arms and stroking her back. "Josh, is everything all right?"

"At this moment life is very good, Mattie," he answered solemnly. "I want to hold you close."

She murmured a satisfied sigh and wriggled closer against him, holding him tightly while he shifted one of his legs between hers.

"I could love you all night. I've lost about three pounds in the past two weeks."

"Let me feel where," she said, her voice filled with contentment while she slid her hands over his buttocks. "You don't have three spare pounds to lose, and I haven't noticed you eating less."

"It isn't from eating or not eating. It's from lack of sleep and exhaustion."

"Sounds like complaints to me."

"Never!" he said, turning and pulling her on top of him as he kissed her and ended the discussion.

The next three days and nights were filled with more parties, and Josh quietly watched Mattie's confidence and joy grow. Now as they dressed for parties, she was bubbly, looking forward to the evening. Josh was aware of several men openly flirting with Mattie. Allen Anderson had been at another of the parties, and his constant attention to Mattie left no doubt in Josh's mind that he was flirting.

Josh was surprised by his reaction. He couldn't remember being disturbed by men's attention to Lisa. The love that had opened in him for Mattie made him want her all to himself. It was something treasured and special that he had never expected to experience again, never in this breathtaking, heart-stopping manner.

Friday night, long after Mattie was asleep, Josh lay staring into the darkness. Heartache tore at him. He wanted to fight for her love, to try to win her over, but all he had to do was remember Lisa. He had done exactly that with Lisa, cajoling her, charming her, arguing with her to stay on the ranch until he lost her forever.

And watching Mattie this week, he knew he had to let her go. She had blossomed since their arrival in Chicago, and excitement hummed in her constantly. She was poised, confident and friendly. She would make a very fine lawyer and she belonged out in the world.

It was as obvious as sunshine that she was having a wonderful time. This woman who had grown up so isolated was a people person. As they rode around town or talked into the night, she told him about the great people she had met. So many names were a blur to him, but Mattie remembered people's names and things about their lives.

On Sunday they would return to the ranch, but he was ready to go now. Every time they made love, he felt more bound to Mattie, and he knew it was going to hurt more to lose her. Knowing he was headed for another terrible heartbreak, he couldn't resist loving her every chance he got. He even thought about selling the ranch and moving to a city to stay with her, but he had to reject that idea. Ranching was his lifeblood. It was all he knew how to do. He was a cowboy, and he had to stay where he was just as surely as she needed to go.

He wanted to be home, to be able to get up and walk outside where he didn't feel closed in. He was tired of Chicago, and he needed the revitalizing that he always found at home on the ranch.

He shifted, looking at Mattie in his arms and wanting her again. It had been less than an hour since they'd made passionate love to each other, yet he wanted to wake her and love her as if it had been more than a year since he'd had the chance.

"Mattie," he whispered, trailing his fingers along her shoulder, feeling his shaft throb and heat burn within him. He leaned over her, brushing kisses across her cheek, down over her shoulder then to her breast. Mattie moaned, wrapped her arms around him, and pulled him over her.

As Josh kissed her fiercely and caressed her until she was gasping, Mattie shifted and curled her hand around his manhood, bending to kiss him. He groaned, his fingers winding tightly in her hair, pulling slightly against her scalp. "Mattie!"

She kissed him, her tongue trailing over the velvet tip of his shaft while she waited to hear a declaration of love. In every way except one, he acted like a man in love. Never once had he said he loved her. Was it all physical? Was it something he didn't want to stop to analyze?

He pulled her up to kiss her, and she stopped wondering about his feelings, locking her arms around him to kiss him as passionately.

It was another hour before they lay quietly in each other's arms again and talked about getting back to the ranch.

The phone rang, and Mattie turned to look at it.

"Mom will answer. Forget it."

"It has to be an emergency for anyone to call at this hour. Suppose it's for you?"

"Why would anyone call me in Chicago? It's probably for Thornton. Forget it."

Mattie snuggled against him, and Josh turned his head to kiss her. Minutes later, she barely heard the knocking at the door until Josh raised his head and she realized she had been hearing the same sound for minutes.

"Damn," Josh said, climbing out of bed and searching for clothes. "Coming!" he called. He yanked on jeans while Mattie picked up her nightgown. As she pulled on a robe, she heard Josh at the door and Sibyl's soft voice.

He closed the door and crossed the room to pick up the phone.

"This is Josh," he said, switching on a small table lamp. The glow highlighted his prominent cheekbones, giving a sheen to his muscles, throwing his cheeks into shadows.

As he listened, his dark gaze swung to Mattie. He closed his eyes momentarily, and she knew something terrible had happened.

Ten

"**M**attie, it's Carlina. It's bad news." Josh held out the phone.

Frowning, Mattie wondered what had happened to her sister. As he handed the receiver to her, Josh put his arm around Mattie and held her close. "Carlina? What's wrong?" Mattie asked.

"Gran died in her sleep tonight," Carlina said in a weepy voice. "She went to sleep and then she was gone."

Mattie drew a deep breath as sorrow filled her. Josh's arm tightened around her waist and she glanced up at him. Tears stung her eyes and she struggled to control her emotions. "I'm glad she was with you. We'll come back home right away."

Josh held her tightly as Mattie stood quietly listening to Carlina. Dazed, Mattie talked about arrangements, watching Josh move away to pull on his T-shirt.

As soon as she told Carlina goodbye and replaced the receiver, Josh crossed the room to enfold her in his arms. "Sorry, honey."

"After we lost Dad, Gran told me that when her time came, we were not to grieve because she had had a long and happy life. I can't keep from grieving, though. I'll miss her."

"I know you will," he said gently, kissing the top of Mattie's head. He held her tightly while she cried against his chest.

"She'll be buried at home in Texas. Josh, I need to get back home."

"I'll change our plane reservations. We can be home tomorrow afternoon. I'll call to make arrangements and then I'll tell Mom." He wiped away her tears with his thumbs and studied her. "Okay?"

"I'm all right."

He picked up the phone, and while she listened to him confirm an early-morning flight, she began to pack to go home to Texas.

Four days later Josh stood beside her in the stifling August heat beneath a thick canopy at the cemetery. Mattie looked at the gravestones. She had now buried her grandparents and her parents. Josh's arm was firmly around her waist, and she felt as if Josh and Elizabeth were her family now. Did Josh feel that way toward her?

As soon as the service ended, friends and relatives came forward to give Mattie and her sisters their condolences. When they returned to Mattie's ranch house, friends and family joined them. Now that Irma was gone, Lottie had moved to Josh's ranch and she had agreed to be a nanny for Elizabeth. She had taken Elizabeth home with her from the reception. It was late that night before Josh and Mattie returned home.

After telling Lottie good-night and looking in on Elizabeth, Josh and Mattie went to the kitchen. He got a cold beer from the refrigerator. "Want a beer?"

Mattie shook her head. "Just a glass of iced tea. I'll get it," she said, kicking off her black pumps and fluffing her hair.

"Mattie, I don't want to rush you, but we ought to talk about the ranch," he said, uncapping the beer. "You're going back in the morning to discuss the ranch with your sisters."

"They want to settle things while they're here so they don't have to come back."

Josh felt a knot in the pit of his stomach. A tiny flame of hope flickered in him, but dread overrode it. He had to face the future, and after Chicago, he could see it all too clearly.

"You said the Rocking R was to be divided three ways, and they've already told you they would like to sell their part."

"Carlina doesn't want to be tied to it in any way. She and Tim said if I can't purchase her share now, they'll wait, take her share of the profits, and let me buy it when I can." Mattie watched Josh shed his suit coat, her body responding to just the sight of him peeling away his jacket and unbuttoning his shirt. Momentarily she forgot everything else except Josh. He wore a navy Western-cut suit and white shirt. Earlier in the evening he had shed his conservative navy tie.

His black boots added to his height. He draped his coat over a chair and unbuttoned his shirt as he hooked his toe below the rung of a chair, pulled it out and sat down.

"What about Andrea?"

"Now that she's engaged, Andrea wants to sell her part because it would pay for the rest of her education. She says she wants me to keep enough to pay me back for supporting her since Dad died, but I told her I didn't want her to do that."

Mattie stirred lemon into the iced tea, sipped it, then went to the table to sit down. "Right now I can't buy their part of the ranch without going into debt again, and I don't want to do that. With our marriage, anything I do will involve you."

"I want to buy their shares and your land, too, if you want to sell it."

Stunned, she stared at him while his offer spun in her mind. Something inside her shattered and crumbled into a sharp pain. Josh was ready to say goodbye. There wouldn't be any reason to make such an offer unless he thought she were leaving—or he wanted her to leave. She felt light-headed and her ears rang.

"Josh, that's a tremendous amount of land," she said without thinking, trying to fill the widening gap of silence. Was he not even considering the possibility that she would stay with him and that her share of land would be joined with his?

"I think I can afford to buy all of the Rocking R. That land adjoins this ranch." Josh watched her while he talked. He hurt and he hoped she never guessed how much. If she had any idea, she would stay with him out of pity and that would be a dreadful mistake.

"I'd like to own the Rocking R land, and this may be the only chance I'll get."

"It'll throw you into debt."

"Nothing I can't handle. I've thought about it, and I'd hate to see it go to someone else. It'll mean tightening up on expenses right now, but in the long run, I think I'll make more money. It'll be worth more. It's good land. The water is better than mine."

They were silent. Mattie knew she should mull over his offer and what it meant to her future, but she didn't want a future away from Josh and Elizabeth. She hadn't expected him to act so swiftly. It looked as if he intended to end their marriage, yet she found that impossible to accept after the past couple of weeks and the intimacy they had shared. Fresh memories taunted her, moments of laughter together, moments in his arms when he sounded as if he loved her and wanted what they had to last forever.

Josh sat sipping the cold beer, not thinking about the offer he had just made. Instead, he was thinking about Mattie, telling himself not to do something to hold her here when she didn't really want to stay. Yet everything in him yearned to do just that. He wanted to pull her onto his lap, kiss her, tell her to stay and forget law school.

"Mattie, according to our prenuptial agreement, I asked you to stay at least one year," Josh said after a length of time.

"I intend to," Mattie replied, her brows arching.

Josh waited, holding his breath, his heart thudding. If she had intentions of staying permanently, now would be the time to tell him. Mattie was as honest and direct as it was possible for a human to be. If she was in love, really in love, and wanted to stay and forget law school, she would tell him. And if she didn't, he had to keep quiet, no matter how painful. He had to let her go.

"I won't hold you to staying the rest of the year," he said, hating what he was doing, yet knowing it was only right and fair to her. He had held one woman with disastrous consequences. He wouldn't make the same mistake twice. If she didn't want to stay, he wouldn't try to keep her here. The bond had to be love, not duty, and it had to be Mattie's choice.

"I know you want to go to law school," Josh continued. "Before you can do anything else, you have to dispose of the ranch. Once you do that, then you can get on with your dreams."

Mattie listened to him, while she felt as if her heart were splintering into a million fragments. Josh was talking calmly about her leaving forever. What about the nights they had spent in each other's arms? The long hours of passionate lovemaking that held so much more for her than just a physical relationship?

She knew he was talking to her, but she didn't hear what he was saying because of the roaring in her ears. With her right hand she clutched the kitchen table and looked down at her left hand in her lap. Her wedding ring glittered, and for the first time its brilliance seemed cold and fragile.

He was making arrangements for her to go. In essence he was telling her goodbye. She felt betrayed, hurt, shocked and yet never once had he said he loved her, she reminded herself. Not one time, even in the throes of passion.

"Mattie?"

She fought tears and hurt and anger. With a supreme effort she looked up and prayed her features were impassive. She could feel the hot sting of tears in her eyes and saw his frown. His dark eyes held an expression of curiosity.

"Sorry, I was thinking about Gran," she lied flatly. She was not going to do something foolish and have him tell her kindly that while he liked her, he didn't love her.

"Oh, sorry. If this is a bad time to talk—"

"No. Carlina leaves tomorrow afternoon so we have to get some decisions made. This will help me," she said. She hoped she made sense. All she could think about was that Josh was saying goodbye. Their interlude was over. She was going to lose him and Elizabeth. Memories of moments with Elizabeth tore at her. Li'l Bit was just beginning to toddle and each day brought wondrous changes. Mattie thought about holding Elizabeth, reading to her, feeling Elizabeth's tiny arms hug her and seeing Elizabeth hold out her arms, wanting Mattie to hold her.

And Josh—she hurt so badly she could barely breathe. Josh was staring at her intently. She looked down at her hand in her lap, turning her engagement ring and looking at the diamond through blurry tears. She should have known he would let her go. From the first moment he had told her—warned her—that he would never get emotionally involved. Her eyes burned with tears, and she wiped at them angrily. "It hurts to lose Gran and the ranch at the same time."

"You don't have to go," he said quietly.

She wanted to scream at him that she wanted his declaration of love to keep her. She wanted Josh and

Elizabeth and not law school! For a moment she felt
like blurting out the truth, but she bit it back, remembering how he had talked about the nannies who had
wanted marriage. He had warned her, clearly, emphatically and often. He had told her marriage made
him feel trapped. Why hadn't she listened?

Unfortunately, she had little control over her heart.
She hurt all over, and she couldn't spend the night
pretending everything was all right or pretending she
still wanted a law career. How long before her control
slipped and she did something foolish that would make
them both miserable?

"Josh, I belong home with my sisters," she said
grimly, knowing she had to get away from him before
she started pleading with him to change his mind.
"I'm going home," she said stiffly, thinking that Josh
and Elizabeth were her only real home.

A muscle worked in his jaw, and his eyes were like
midnight. He nodded and she turned, yanking up her
purse and rushing to get some clothes.

Josh sat in the empty kitchen. He felt as if his world
had ended. How would he exist without her? If he
bought her ranch, there would be little chance to turn
around, sell out and move to a city to stay with her.
And he couldn't do that even if he saw a way. He
belonged on the ranch as surely as Mattie belonged in
a law firm in a city.

But he loved her and wanted her. She was leaving
him right now. He could feel it in his bones. He could
have held her to the agreement to stay the rest of the
year. Maybe by that time she would want to stay forever, but after the week in Chicago he knew he had
to let her go, no matter what he felt. He glanced over

his shoulder at the doorway, thinking about her gathering her things to go. She was leaving him, but right now she was still under his roof. And he knew she was still susceptible to his kisses.

Angrily he shoved back the chair and strode through the house. He found her in his room. Her back was to him and she was folding a pair of jeans. With a pounding heart he crossed the room and turned her to face him.

"Josh—"

He bent his head, his mouth coming down on her soft lips while he kissed her. Startled, Mattie wrapped her arms around his neck. Her heart thudded and she wondered about his feelings. He was kissing her as if he wanted to hold her forever.

And she wanted him forever. Tears stung and fell unheeded as she returned his kisses. His lips were rough on hers; his tongue thrust deeply into her mouth. With each thrust and stroke of his tongue, she felt puzzled. If he was letting her go, why was he kissing her as though he couldn't bear to say goodbye?

As abruptly as he had pulled her into his arms, he released her. "Go ahead, Mattie," he said, his voice cold and flat. He turned and left the room, and she stared at the empty doorway. He had to feel something strong for her to storm in and kiss her like that. Yet he had told her to go.

With shaking hands she grabbed up some of her things, knowing she could return and get the rest when she had her emotions more under control. She went to Elizabeth's room and bent over the baby bed to brush wispy hair away from her cheek. She longed to pick the child up and hold her close, to feel Elizabeth's little arms around her neck again. Tears streamed down her cheeks as she stroked and patted Elizabeth.

"I'll miss you terribly, Li'l Bit. Your daddy knows what he wants, though. He loves you so much, and he'll always take care of you, and I'll always think of you. I love you, sweetie. I love you so much, Elizabeth."

Mattie leaned down to hug Elizabeth, then left swiftly, almost running to the truck, while everything in her screamed to go back and tell Josh she loved him.

Let him send her away if he wanted to. All she had to do was remember his contempt of the nannies who wanted to be his wife and she kept going to the truck. She didn't want his sympathy or his contempt.

With tears flowing, Mattie climbed inside the pickup. Where was Josh? He was not coming out to stop her. She slammed the door of the truck and started the motor, rushing down the road to drive home. When she reached the highway, she pulled over to cry, letting go all her pent-up emotions. She hurt and she wanted more than anything this man who had become the world to her.

It was almost an hour later before she reached her ranch, then tiptoed to her own room, closed the door and sat down near a window to stare into the night. She couldn't sleep, her mind racing. He had acted like a man in love. Had their lovemaking meant so little to him? Should she go back, tell him she loved him, that she wanted to try to make their marriage last?

Everything in her cried out to do that, yet Josh's coldness held her immobile. If he loved her, he would have told her. If he wanted her, he never would have let her go.

She could remember how he had swept her into this marriage over all her protests and doubts. If he wanted her now, he would be declaring it and fighting to get her to stay. Except he wouldn't have to fight at all. She covered her eyes to cry again.

The next morning as she drank hot coffee, Carlina's husband, Tim, was the first downstairs. "Morning, Mattie. Didn't expect to find you here," he said, giving her a long look. She knew it was obvious she had been crying, but she barely knew her brother-in-law and he didn't question her. He wore chinos and a tan shirt and loafers. His black hair was cut just below his ears and was neatly parted and combed. She wondered if he was impatient to get back to Denver and his brokerage business.

"I know Carlina and Andrea want to settle the question of the ranch while all of you are here," she said to him.

"It'll make it a lot easier. I talked to your husband yesterday, and it sounds as if he wants to buy our share and Andrea's."

"That's right."

"Good morning. I thought I heard voices," Andrea's fiancé, Chet Holden, said, raking his blond hair back from his face as he entered the room. He was only inches taller than Andrea, several inches shorter than Mattie, but his ready smile always made her feel at ease with him.

The men moved around the kitchen getting orange juice and coffee, and she thought how different they were. Chet was short, blond and worked with computers. Tim was a stockbroker, as tall as Mattie, and he always seemed slightly preoccupied when she was around him as if he were still thinking about his business. She wondered what they thought of Josh with his long shaggy hair and country background.

Before she could ponder the matter further, both sisters entered the room.

"What are you doing here?" Carlina asked, stretching and yawning. She wore pink sweats and was barefoot as she stared at Mattie with curiosity.

Andrea was in boxer shorts and a T-shirt. Her tousled mop of curls was in a tangle as she stared owlishly at Mattie while she poured a glass of orange juice.

"I needed to talk to you about the ranch," Mattie said, removing slices of golden toast from the toaster to set them on the table. While they ate breakfast of fruit and toast and hot coffee, they discussed the disposal of the ranch.

After they finished their conversation, Tim called Josh and made an appointment to meet with him at Josh's office at his place. Next Tim made an appointment with an appraiser.

Over an hour later everyone left except Andrea, who sat at the kitchen table with Mattie. "Why are you home?"

Mattie shook her hair away from her face and looked out the kitchen window. She dreaded telling Andrea the truth, but there was no way to avoid it. "Josh and I had a marriage of convenience, nothing more."

"Get outta here! I don't believe it, Mattie!"

Mattie faced her sister, looking into concerned blue eyes as she nodded. "It's true."

"Nobody does that!"

"I did it. He needed someone for Elizabeth, and he agreed to pay the debts Dad had incurred among other things. I told him before we ever went into it that if something happened to Gran, I wanted to sell the ranch and go to law school."

Andrea's jaw dropped. "No! You love this place."

For a moment Mattie felt a flicker of amusement. "Of course I love our home, but I don't want to be tied to it any more than you do. Do you want to live here and run it?"

"No, but I wouldn't know how. You do. It's all you've ever done."

"But it's not all I ever want to do," Mattie said patiently.

"All those years with Dad—you were unhappy?"

"No, but Dad's gone and I want something else."

"Does Carlina know?"

"Not yet. I'll tell her this morning, but I didn't want to announce it with Tim and Chet here."

"You want to go to law school?"

"I've already been accepted. If I get going and leave the details of selling the ranch to Tim—who seems willing to take charge—I can start this semester. School begins a week from Monday. I'd like to leave for Austin this afternoon to look for an apartment. Then I'll be back by Friday at the latest."

"You waited to do this because of Dad and Gran, didn't you?"

"Yes."

"Have you wanted to get away as much as Carlina and I did?"

"No. I like it here, but I want another career," she said, thinking about Josh and Elizabeth. "I don't want to live alone in this house and run this ranch by myself."

"And you don't have a real marriage?"

"It's real enough as far as the law is concerned, but we'll end it now."

"You had that big wedding because of Gran, didn't you?"

"Yes," Mattie answered, aware Andrea was studying her intently.

"If you want to go to law school, why do you look like you've been crying?"

Mattie drew a deep breath. Trust her little sis to notice something was amiss. She stood and moved to the window, looking outside and struggling to control her emotions. "I love him, Andrea."

"Well, for heaven's sake, why are you leaving?"

"He wants me to." Mattie wiped her eyes and turned around. "He had nannies who wanted to marry him before our arrangement and he told me he could never love anyone again and they made him feel trapped. I'm not trapping him into a marriage he doesn't want."

Andrea stood and crossed the room to hug her sister. "Maybe if you stayed longer, he'd fall in love. He married you. Surely you talked about it lasting longer than this."

"I don't want him wishing he could get rid of me."

"He didn't look like he wanted to get rid of you." Andrea leaned back to study Mattie, looking up at her intently. "He seemed to care a lot, Mattie. It didn't look like an act, either."

"He didn't ask me to stay."

"I think you ought to go back and talk it over with him."

"Andrea, he knows what he wants. And he doesn't hesitate to say what he wants."

"He might be waiting for you to make the first move."

"He's not the type."

"Let's go talk to Carlina."

Nodding, Mattie knew she had to tell both sisters. Chet and Tim passed them on the stairs as they left to meet with Josh, and by the time the sisters reached Carlina's room, they had the house to themselves.

Only half listening, Mattie answered Carlina's questions about her plans. Then she listened as Andrea told Carlina that Mattie was in love with Josh, but leaving because he hadn't asked her to stay.

"I think she should go back and talk it over with him," Andrea said.

"I don't," Carlina snapped. "Men can be so obtuse. And if you want something else besides life on a ranch, here's your chance."

"I don't think you're right," Andrea argued, and Mattie wondered if they had forgotten her presence.

"Yes, I am." She glanced at Mattie. "You two seemed a mismatch anyway. I'd say go for law school. You'll meet the right guy there."

Mattie listened to them argue over her, but her thoughts were on Josh. She stood and headed toward the door. "I'm going to dress and leave for Austin. I'll think about what you said, Andrea, but it won't hurt to go look at apartments. And promise me, both of you, that you will not lecture Josh or tell him I'm in love with him or anything like that.''

''I don't want to promise,'' Andrea said with a pout. ''Maybe he just needs a nudge.''

''Andrea, he isn't the kind of man to nudge.''

''She's right. I promise,'' Carlina said.

''I promise, but I think you're making a big mistake,'' Andrea added, and Mattie knew she could count on them keeping their word.

All the time she bathed and changed and packed, she thought about Josh and Elizabeth and Andrea's arguments. And Carlina's belief that they were a mismatched pair. She hadn't felt mismatched. With Josh she had felt complete—a desirable woman.

She kissed her sisters goodbye and climbed into the car that was so seldom used since her father's death. As she turned onto the highway, she glanced down the road toward Josh's. It was another hot day with unusually high winds.

She sped along, barely noticing the landscape, her thoughts were still on Josh. Should she tell him that she loved him and would rather stay with him and Elizabeth, even if he didn't love her in return? He acted like a man in love, and maybe she was making a dreadful mistake. She didn't want law school. She wanted Josh and Elizabeth.

Mattie spent the next two days looking at apartments near the university. On Saturday morning she found one she liked, but she didn't make a decision to sign a lease. Instead she went back to the motel to think about her future.

As she unlocked the door the phone was ringing. She rushed across the room and yanked up the receiver. ''Hello.''

''Mattie?''

At the sound of Josh's bass voice, her heart missed a beat. She clung to the phone, closed her eyes and sat on the edge of the bed. ''I just came in,'' she said breathlessly. How wonderful his voice sounded! Why was he calling her? Was he going to tell her to come home?

''Carlina said you're apartment hunting,'' he said quietly. She clutched the phone, words tumbling in her mind. Should she tell him she wanted to go back to the ranch? Back to him and Elizabeth?

''Yes, but I haven't found anything.''

''We miss you,'' he said in the same tone of voice that sounded withdrawn and controlled.

''I miss you terribly,'' she admitted. Silence stretched between them. *Say you want me to come home.* She knew the silence was becoming awkward, yet she was afraid to speak.

Josh leaned back in the chair with his feet propped on the desk. He gripped the phone until his knuckles were white and his heart thudded with her last words. He waited, hoping, hurting, wanting her to say she was coming home. Her sister Carlina had said Mattie was filled with plans for law school and apartment hunting, and he had spent the past sleepless nights telling himself she was gone for good. Yet her statement that she missed him terribly didn't sound as though she was completely wrapped up in the idea of law school.

He rubbed his bristly jaw. He hadn't bothered to shave the past few days. He went through the motions

of trying to work and knew the men were giving him
room and leaving him alone. Lottie cheerfully cared
for Elizabeth and talked about when Mattie would be
back home. He didn't care to discuss with Lottie that
Mattie would not be returning to stay, so he had listened without comment.

And this morning he could stand it no longer without at least talking to Mattie. He couldn't resist calling
her. Her statement surprised him. Hope spread in him
like light filling a dark room. *I miss you terribly.* What
did that mean? He was conscious of the lengthening
silence and he waited for more from her.

"Mattie, we're working out details for me to buy
the Rocking R. Andrea said you'll be home tomorrow."

"That's right." Tears flowed unheeded. She wanted
his arms around her, wanted his loving. *Please say you
want me to come home.*

"I'll see you when you get home."

"Sure. I wish I could talk to Elizabeth."

"She keeps calling for you," he said gruffly, and
Mattie felt her heart constrict.

"Tell her I miss her."

"Sure. See you tomorrow, Mattie."

"I'm glad you called."

"So am I. It's good to talk." He replaced the receiver and ran his hand across his eyes. He loved her
with all his being and he wanted her home. It tore him
to pieces when Elizabeth started crying for Mattie.
And the long lonely nights in his empty bed were pure
hell. He swung his feet to the floor and put his head
in his hands.

Restlessly he stood and went to the window to look

outside without seeing anything except Mattie's big green eyes. "Hellfire," he said, clamping his jaw shut tightly. His eyes narrowed. Mattie was mature, intelligent and forthright. She said she missed him terribly. He clenched his fists, feeling his resolve crumble.

Just once, he was going to tell the woman he loved her. If she said she wanted out of his life and out of the marriage, then he'd let her go, but he was going to let her know what she meant to him. He took a deep breath, feeling an urgent need to tell her now. He wasn't going to wait for her to come home before he told her. If Lottie would stay tonight with Elizabeth, he was going to drive to Austin now.

Excitement and hope flickered to life in him, and he strode out of the room. "Lottie!"

Eleven

Josh ran to his room and laid out a fresh pair of jeans. He yanked off his shirt to shower. As he crossed the room, the phone rang and he picked up the receiver.

As soon as he answered, he heard the sheriff's clipped voice. "Josh, it's Zach Burnett. We just got a call. Someone on the highway spotted smoke. It's your land. I'm headed that way now."

As Josh listened, he moved to the window. An icy tremor raked him when he saw the dark column of smoke that stretched broadly above the treetops and rose skyward where it spread and dissipated.

"We have rain predicted," Zach continued, "and it's dark to the north, but no rain will be here in the next few hours. The smoke was to the southwest of your place, and we've got a hellacious south wind blowing now. I'll notify as many as I can to get you help. Fire departments from three towns are already on the way.''

''Thanks, I'm going.''

The line went dead as Josh dashed down the hall and met Dusty coming toward him. Dusty's boots scraped the floor. He had dirt on his jeans and smudges on his shirt. One look in his gray eyes, and Josh knew they were in deep trouble.

''The place is on fire. We're moving the animals. The way this wind's blowing, your house and everything will be in its path.''

''I just talked to Zach Burnett. I'll be there as soon as I can,'' Josh said to Dusty, who had already turned around and headed for the door. Lottie stood in the family room doorway.

''Lottie, go down to your house and get what you need. Get your car. I'll pack Li'l Bit's things and you take her to town. Get a room at the hotel and tell them to put it on my bill. Hurry quick! You two need to get out of here. The fire is damned close.''

Desperate to get Elizabeth out of harm's way, he picked her up, hugging her before he set her down in her room. ''You and Lottie are going in the car, sweetie. I'm going to put your things in your bag,'' he said, yanking open drawers and flinging Elizabeth's clothes into a bag. He raced to his room and grabbed another bag, running back to jam it full of her clothing and toys and books. He packed Lisa's picture and a baby picture of Elizabeth.

''Mr. Brand, I'm ready,'' Lottie said, coming into the room.

''Look and see if I've left anything you need. I'll put these bags in your car, Lottie.'' He yanked up two

stuffed bears and a favorite blanket before dashing to
Lottie's car. When he stepped outside, a warm gust of
wind buffeted him and he could smell the fire.

He felt a flicker of relief when he saw the barn
standing open and empty. Lottie came out carrying
Elizabeth and two sacks. He took the sacks that were
filled with bottles and formula and set them in the car,
then he took Elizabeth and buckled her into the car
seat. "Thanks, Lottie. Say a prayer for us."

"I will, Mr. Brand. You be careful. Fires are mean.
Thank goodness we're supposed to get rain, and it
looks dark to the north."

He glanced toward the south and then looked at the
smoke. "I don't think we're going to get it in time to
help save this place."

She climbed into the car while he leaned down to
kiss Elizabeth. "You're my sweetie. I'll see you tonight, Li'l Bit. Be Daddy's good girl, okay?"

"Bye, bye," she said, touching his cheek and smiling at him.

"Take care, Lottie." He closed the car door and
turned to run for his pickup, racing around the barn
and then leaving the road to cut across the open field
toward a stand of oaks.

Mattie raced along the highway and then slowed as
she drove through Latimer. She was going home to
Josh. He would have to tell her to go. They had been
honest enough with each other that she knew he would
say what he truly felt. And when she remembered
things he had said in the past and his words on the
phone this morning, she thought their marriage had a
chance. And that was all she prayed for. If he would

just give her a chance, just go back to what they had, because that was incredibly special to her.

After talking to him, she had sat for thirty minutes debating what she wanted to do, then had decided to go home. She'd checked out of the motel, packed and left Austin. Now she was so close and her pulse raced eagerly.

She was just out of Latimer when she topped a hill and saw the billowing smoke in the distance. The black column rose and spread across the sky above the treetops, and she turned icy. It probably was much farther away than it appeared, she reassured herself. But with every mile closer, she grew more worried. She prayed silently that the ranches would be all right.

Pressing her foot on the accelerator, she sped along, passing the turn to the Rocking R. With every mile her fright grew. Now she could see the tips of orange flames leaping above treetops. She wondered how far she could drive before she had to turn back. She wouldn't drive into smoke. She prayed it was beyond Josh's place, far from his house and buildings, but she could tell it was close.

Her fear became sheer terror when she neared the road to his house. She could see the flames roaring through trees, black smoke billowing. Gray smoke that had thinned rolled over the car and cinders blew through the air. The acrid smell stung her throat, but in spite of the danger, she turned down his road and raced to the house. She could see men in the distance fighting the fire. A pumper truck drove along the burning edge, the thick stream of silvery water shooting from the fireman's hose looking too inadequate for the raging inferno.

She knew Josh would be fighting the fire, but where were Lottie and Li'l Bit? Storm clouds gathered to the north and Mattie prayed that rain would come soon.

She braked near the back door and flung herself out of the car. The barn stood empty, and she realized the animals had been moved. She rushed inside the house.

"Lottie!"

There was only silence. Mattie yanked down keys to the other pickup and raced into the family room. Something should be saved for Josh. His great-grandfather, grandfather and father had passed furnishings down to him. She grabbed the rifle above the mantel and removed a lamp from the small table his great-grandfather had made, then carried them to the pickup. She raced inside for more.

Each trip out to the pickup, the fire moved closer. Men were yelling. The rumble and crackle of the flames were loud when she couldn't cram another item into the pickup. The last armload was filled with trash bags of Josh's boots and clothing and guns, pictures she had found in his closet—their wedding pictures.

She slid behind the wheel and raced away from the house, driving down the highway. She sped home to get her own pickup and then rushed back to help fight the fire.

Leaving the pickup parked on the highway, she grabbed the shovel from the back. A gust of warm air struck her and then another gust that was cool, and she looked at the storm clouds racing overhead. Rain was coming, but it was going to be too late. She ran toward the fire, seeing a stranger swinging a wet gunnysack and beating out flames.

Someone had turned over the ground so a wide lane

of dirt made a firebreak, and she prayed the fire couldn't jump it.

She began to dig, throwing dirt on the flames, trying to smother the fire. Flames licked at her, and the heat poured over her in waves while smoke made her cough. It stung her eyes and throat, and in minutes the world was blurred as her eyes watered.

The house was a quarter of a mile away but in clear view, and she watched in horror as the roof burst into flames. Cinders must have blown and fallen on the shingle roof. In seconds it was a raging fire.

As the orange fire licked across the roof, she ached. For Josh, for his monetary loss, but much more for the loss of a home that had been passed down from generation to generation, one that he treasured. She turned back to fighting the fire that had become a dim blur as tears filled her eyes.

She felt the wind shift only seconds after she heard a man nearby give a triumphant whoop. In minutes the fire was blowing back on itself, back over land burned to ashes. Her shoulders throbbed, her hands stung and her arms ached as she paused and wiped perspiration from her forehead. She turned to look at the house that was burning.

Fire raged through the structure. The windows and roof were gone. The place was a raging inferno. Fire trucks pumped water on the flames that burned out of control. Nearby, through the smoke, one of the men strode toward her. His T-shirt was blackened and ripped, a jagged tear across the shoulder. His jeans were covered with mud and soot. As he approached, she recognized the familiar long stride and broad shoulders. Her heart thudded, and she threw aside the shovel and ran toward him. ''Josh!''

Twelve

Josh's strong arms wrapped around her as he bent his head to kiss her hungrily. His jaw was bristly, scraping her face, but she was barely aware of it. Trembling with joy, she held him tightly. Hot tears spilled down her cheeks, mingling with their kisses while she returned Josh's kiss, wanting him so badly, wanting him forever.

"Your house," she whispered, leaning back.

"I was coming to Austin today when the fire stopped me. Why are you here?"

Her heart leaped when he said he'd been going to Austin. "Josh, I—"

He kissed her again before she could say more—another hungry, passionate kiss that made her forget everything else momentarily.

Josh held her, his heart pounding. As long as he

lived he would never forget the moment Dusty said he had seen Mattie fighting the fire. He wasn't going to let her go this time without a fight. Mattie wasn't Lisa. She was a different woman; theirs were different circumstances, and she was going to have to make the choice. Right now he couldn't get enough of her, kissing her wildly, wanting to touch every inch of her. He wanted to possess her, to hold her, to bind her to him completely.

He raised his head. "I love you, Mattie," he said firmly.

Mattie's heart turned over, and everything inside her melted into a warmth that shook her. "I came back because I want our marriage."

"Thank God!" he exclaimed, and bent his head to kiss her again. This time, as she clung to him, her heart pounded with fierce joy. A twinge of guilt reminded her of the fire. She had no right to feel delirious with happiness when his house had burned to the ground.

Just then the first big drops of rain hit them, but Josh barely noticed. He framed her face with his hands. "I love you, Mattie. I want you and our marriage, too. I've been in hell without you."

She touched his jaw while her joy grew. Her heart pounded with delight over his declaration of love. "Josh, I've always loved you. Always."

He gave her a crooked smile. "I'll settle for now, lady."

"I guess it took my going away for you to realize—"

"The hell it did. I've been in love with you almost since our wedding. I didn't realize my own feelings at first, but then I knew."

"Why didn't you tell me?" she asked, frowning and wondering why a man so direct in everything else would keep what he felt in his heart to himself.

"I was going to tell you when we went to Chicago, and then I saw you take to all those people and city life like a duck to water. You belong in that environment, Mattie. You have the brains and the personality—"

"Oh, my! Josh, stop! As far as taking to city life and wanting to be a lawyer—oh, darlin', it's you and Elizabeth I want."

Anything else she was going to say left her mind as he tightened his arms around her again and kissed her hard. She returned his kisses until they were both breathing hard.

She looked at him in disbelief, remembering the solemn moments and desperate lovemaking in Chicago and now understanding what was tearing at him. "All because of the Chicago trip, you kept quiet?"

He looked at her solemnly again. "That and another reason. If I had tried to hold you here when you wanted to go, I was afraid it would have been like Lisa all over again. Staying here when she wanted to leave is what killed her."

"Oh, Josh! I'm not Lisa. And I can survive coming back to the ranch."

"I decided that today. That's why I was going to Austin. I had gone to shower when I got a call from Zach that someone spotted the fire."

"As much as I want to be alone with you, we better join the others," she said, trying to be practical, when all she wanted to do was hold him and kiss him. "I'm so sorry about your house."

214   HER TORRID TEMPORARY MARRIAGE

"That's not important next to getting you back," he said solemnly, his dark eyes seeming to draw her to his soul. "You gave me back life and love, Mattie. I hope I can repay you even half as much as what you've given to me and Elizabeth."

She placed her palm against his cheek as tears stung her eyes. "I love you, Josh Brand."

He kissed her hand and glanced over his shoulder at the house. "We'll rebuild, Mattie. Maybe it was time to let go of the past."

Big drops of rain fell faster, and Josh looked at his burning land. The fire was dying now as the wind blew from the north and swept what flames were left back on scorched ground, but his house was a smoldering ruin. He placed his Stetson on Mattie's head and she looked up at him.

The skies opened and rain poured over them, drenching them and plastering Mattie's blouse to her body. It was cold, a hissing downpour. Mattie never remembered rain looking so wonderful to her before.

"I've got to thank everyone for helping," Josh said, his arms still tight around her waist. "And then I want you alone, all to myself. We need to plan a honeymoon."

"We can take Elizabeth if you want."

He shook his head. "Li'l Bit and Lottie get along fabulously and Mom would like to keep her, too. Li'l Bit will probably get a week with Mom, and Lottie can have a week's vacation. And I'll have you in my bed, all to myself."

Mattie's body tingled in response to his words, and she felt like laughing with bubbly joy. "I can't wait! Let's go. I'll help you thank people. Josh, I saved what

I could from the house. It's in my pickup at my place.''

"Ah, Mattie, thank you,'' he said. "We left in such a rush. You didn't happen to save any other clothes of mine, did you?''

"Of course,'' she answered smugly. "The way I figure it, you can't get along without me, Josh Brand!''

"Damn straight, I can't. And I don't intend to try again.''

Mattie stood on a balcony and looked at the sparkling lights of Paris, the Arc de Triomphe in one direction, the Eiffel Tower in another. A hand locked around her belt, and she was pulled back through glass doors into the hotel bedroom.

"Hey!''

"Come here,'' Josh said, both of them tumbling across the bed as she fell into his arms. "You can look at Paris anytime.'' He sobered and stared at her. "You like cities, Mattie. You love it here. I'll tell you, woman, I'm going to do everything I can to keep you on that ranch in Texas!''

"Really? And what are you going to do to keep me there?'' she teased in a sultry voice. His chest expanded and his hand covered the back of her head as he pulled her down to kiss her. He rolled over her, shifting to try to unbutton her blouse while she unfastened his belt. While Josh kissed and caressed her, their clothing was tossed aside. Mattie stroked him, her fingers closing around his throbbing shaft. She thrilled to his groan of pleasure.

He shifted over her, moving between her thighs until he lowered himself and entered her. Eager, wanting him more each time they were together, she wrapped her legs around him, her hands digging into his firm buttocks. She moved with him until she splintered into a blinding release.

"I love you, woman. Love you so damned much," he said in a gruff, husky voice, turning his head to look at her.

She gazed into his dark eyes as she ran her fingertips over his chest. "Josh, I'd like to get off the Pill. I'm twenty-eight. I know you have terrible expenses with the house gone and buying my sisters' shares of our place—"

He placed his finger on her lips. "Shh," he said, kissing her lightly, showering kisses on her temple, her cheeks, her throat. "I think that's a grand idea, Mattie. You're wonderful with Elizabeth. And Elizabeth would be delighted to have a little sibling. And I'd love another child. We'll manage. We've got my cattle and your cattle, and I can sell off some. Hell, I can sell part of the land, and we'll still have more than either of us had a year ago. We'll manage." He looked into her eyes. "I love you."

She wrapped her arms around his neck as he leaned over to kiss her again. Mattie closed her eyes and returned his kisses, holding him, knowing she loved Josh and Elizabeth more than anything or anyone in the world. And hopefully soon there would be another little Brand to love!

* * * * *

Silhouette®

Where love comes alive™

SILHOUETTE *Romance*™

From first love to forever, these love stories are
for today's woman with traditional values.

Silhouette® *Desire*

A highly passionate, emotionally powerful
and always provocative read.

Silhouette®

SPECIAL EDITION™

Emotional, compelling stories that capture the
intensity of living, loving and creating a family in
today's world.

Silhouette®

INTIMATE MOMENTS™

A roller-coaster read that delivers romantic thrills
in a world of suspense, adventure and more.

Visit Silhouette at www.eHarlequin.com

SDIR2

SILHOUETTE *Romance*™

Escape to a place where a kiss is still a kiss...
Feel the breathless connection...
Fall in love as though it were
the very first time...
Experience the power of love!

Come to where favorite authors—such as
**Diana Palmer, Stella Bagwell,
Marie Ferrarella** and many more—
deliver heart-warming romance and genuine
emotion, time after time after time....

Silhouette Romance—
stories straight from the heart!

Silhouette®
Where love comes alive™

eHARLEQUIN.com

Looking for today's most popular
books at great prices?
At www.eHarlequin.com, we offer:

- An **extensive selection** of romance
  books by top authors!

- **New** releases, Themed Collections
  and hard-to-find **backlist.**

- A sneak peek at Upcoming books.

- Enticing book **excerpts** and **back
  cover copy!**

- Read recommendations from other
  readers (and post your own)!

- Find out what everybody's reading
  in **Bestsellers.**

- **Save BIG** with everyday discounts
  and exclusive online offers!

- Easy, convenient **24-hour shopping.**

- Our **Romance Legend** will help select
  reading that's *exactly* right for you!

**Your purchases are 100%
guaranteed—so shop online
at www.eHarlequin.com today!**